"Due to recent disruptions in the fabric of our worlds, beings have been released who would not otherwise have the power they now possess. And possessing great power, they crave for more—for all the power that there is in our universe . . . They are outside the power of any of our gods, so a more powerful group has been summoned—yourselves. The Champion Eternal in four of his incarnations (and four is the maximum number we can risk without precipitating further unwelcome disruptions among the planes of Earth)—Erekose, Elric, Corum, and Hawkmoon . . ."

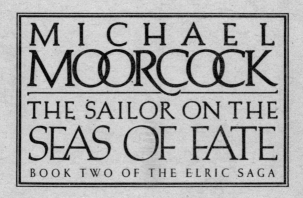

MICHAEL MOORCOCK

THE SAILOR ON THE
SEAS OF FATE

BOOK TWO OF THE ELRIC SAGA

BERKLEY BOOKS, NEW YORK

*For Bill Butler, Mike and
Tony, and all at Unicorn
Books, Wales.*

This Berkley Book contains the complete
text of the original edition.

THE SAILOR ON THE SEAS OF FATE

A Berkley Book / published by arrangement with
the author

PRINTING HISTORY
DAW Books edition / December 1976
Berkley edition / July 1983
Second printing / November 1983
Third printing / March 1984
Fourth printing / July 1984

ISBN: 0-425-07686-5

Book ONE

SAILING TO THE FUTURE

*. . . and leaving his cousin Yyrkoon sitting
as regent upon the Ruby Throne of Melniboné,
leaving his cousin Cymoril weeping for him
and despairing of his ever returning, Elric sailed
from Imrryr, the Dreaming City, and went to
seek an unknown goal in the worlds of the
Young Kingdoms where Melnibonéans were, at
best, disliked.*

*—THE CHRONICLE OF THE
BLACK SWORD*

It was as if the man stood in a vast cavern whose walls
and roof were comprised of gloomy, unstable colors which
would occasionally break and admit rays of light from the
moon. That these walls were mere clouds massed above
mountains and ocean was hard to believe, for all that the
moonlight pierced them, stained them and revealed the
black and turbulent sea washing the shore on which the
man now stood.

Distant thunder rolled; distant lightning flickered. A
thin rain fell. And the clouds were never still. From dusky
jet to deadly white they swirled slowly, like the cloaks of
men and women engaged in a trancelike and formalistic
minuet: the man standing on the shingle of the grim beach
was reminded of giants dancing to the music of the far-
away storm and felt as one must feel who walks unwit-
tingly into a hall where the gods are at play. He turned
his gaze from the clouds to the ocean.

The sea seemed weary. Great waves heaved themselves

together with difficulty and collapsed as if in relief, gasping as they struck sharp rocks.

The man pulled his hood closer about his face and he looked over his leathern shoulder more than once as he trudged closer to the sea and let the surf spill upon the toes of his knee-length black boots. He tried to peer into the cavern formed by the clouds but could see only a short distance. There was no way of telling what lay on the other side of the ocean or, indeed, how far the water extended. He put his head on one side, listening carefully, but could hear nothing but the sounds of the sky and the sea. He sighed. For a moment a moonbeam touched him and from the white flesh of his face there glowed two crimson, tormented eyes; then darkness came back. Again the man turned, plainly fearing that the light had revealed him to some enemy. Making as little sound as possible, he headed toward the shelter of the rocks on his left.

Elric was tired. In the city of Ryfel in the land of Pikarayd he had naïvely sought acceptance by offering his services as a mercenary in the army of the governor of that place. For his foolishness he had been imprisoned as a Melnibonéan spy (it was obvious to the governor that Elric could be nothing else) and had but recently escaped with the aid of bribes and some minor sorcery.

The pursuit, however, had been almost immediate. Dogs of great cunning had been employed and the governor himself had led the hunt beyond the borders of Pikarayd and into the lonely, uninhabited shale valleys of a world locally called the Dead Hills, in which little grew or tried to live.

Up the steep sides of small mountains, whose slopes consisted of gray, crumbling slate, which made a clatter to be heard a mile or more away, the white-faced one had ridden. Along dales all but grassless and whose river-bottoms had seen no water for scores of years, through cave-tunnels bare of even a stalactite, over plateaus from which rose cairns of stones erected by a forgotten folk, he had sought to escape his pursuers, and soon it seemed to him that he had left the world he knew forever, that he had crossed a supernatural frontier and had arrived in one of those bleak places of which he had read in the legends of his people, where once Law and Chaos had fought each other to a stalemate, leaving their battleground empty of life and the possibility of life.

And at last he had ridden his horse so hard that its heart had burst and he had abandoned its corpse and continued on foot, panting to the sea, to this narrow beach, unable to go farther forward and fearing to return lest his enemies should be lying in wait for him.

He thought that he would give much for a boat now. It would not be long before the dogs discovered his scent and led their masters to the beach. He shrugged. Best to die here alone, perhaps, slaughtered by those who did not even know his name. His only regret would be that Cymoril would wonder why he had not returned at the end of the year.

He had no food and few of the drugs which had of late sustained his energy. Without renewed energy he could not contemplate working a sorcery which might conjure for him some means of crossing the sea and making, perhaps, for the Isle of the Purple Towns where the people were least unfriendly to Melnibonéans.

It had been only a month since he had left behind his court and his queen-to-be, letting Yyrkoon sit on the throne of Melniboné until his return. He had thought he might learn more of the human folk of the Young Kingdoms by mixing with them, but they had rejected him either with outright hatred or wary and insincere humility. Nowhere had he found one willing to believe that a Melnibonéan (and they did not know he was the emperor) would willingly throw in his lot with the human beings who had once been in thrall to that cruel and ancient race. And now, as he stood beside a bleak sea feeling trapped and already defeated, he knew himself to be alone in a malevolent universe, bereft of friends and purpose, a useless, sickly anachronism, a fool brought low by his own insufficiencies of character, by his profound inability to believe wholly in the rightness or the

wrongness of anything at all. He lacked faith in his race,
in his birthright, in gods or men, and above all he lacked
faith in himself.

His pace slackened; his hand fell upon the pommel
of his black runesword Stormbringer, the blade which
had so recently defeated its twin, Mournblade, in the
fleshy chamber within a sunless world of Limbo. Stormbringer, seemingly half-sentient, was now his only companion, his only confidant, and it had become his neurot-
ic habit to talk to the sword as another might talk to his
horse or as a prisoner might share his thoughts with a
cockroach in his cell.

"Well, Stormbringer, shall we walk into the sea and
end it now?" His voice was dead, barely a whisper. "At
least we shall have the pleasure of thwarting those who
follow us."

He made a halfhearted movement toward the sea, but
to his fatigued brain it seemed that the sword murmured,
stirred against his hip, pulled back. The albino chuckled.
"You exist to live and to take lives. Do I exist, then, to
die and bring both those I love and hate the mercy of
death? Sometimes I think so. A sad pattern, if that should
be the pattern. Yet there must be more to all this. . . ."

He turned his back upon the sea, peering upward at
the monstrous clouds forming and reforming above his
head, letting the light rain fall upon his face, listening to
the complex, melancholy music which the sea made as it
washed over rocks and shingle and was carried this way
and that by conflicting currents. The rain did little to
refresh him. He had not slept at all for two nights and
had slept hardly at all for several more. He must have
ridden for almost a week before his horse collapsed.

At the base of a damp granite crag which rose nearly
thirty feet above his head, he found a depression in the
ground in which he could squat and be protected from
the worst of the wind and the rain. Wrapping his heavy
leather cloak tightly about him, he eased himself into
the hole and was immediately asleep. Let them find him
while he slept. He wanted no warning of his death.

Harsh, gray light struck his eyes as he stirred. He raised his neck, holding back a groan at the stiffness of his muscles, and he opened his eyes. He blinked. It was morning—perhaps even later, for the sun was invisible —and a cold mist covered the beach. Through the mist the darker clouds could still be seen above, increasing the effect of his being inside a huge cavern. Muffled a little, the sea continued to splash and hiss, though it seemed calmer than it had on the previous night, and there were now no sounds of a storm. The air was very cold.

Elric began to stand up, leaning on his sword for support, listening carefully, but there was no sign that his enemies were close by. Doubtless they had given up the chase, perhaps after finding his dead horse.

He reached into his belt pouch and took from it a sliver of smoked bacon and a vial of yellowish liquid. He sipped from the vial, replaced the stopper, and returned the vial to his pouch as he chewed on the meat. He was thirsty. He trudged farther up the beach and found a pool of rainwater not too tainted with salt. He drank his fill, staring around him. The mist was fairly thick and if he moved too far from the beach he knew he would become immediately lost. Yet did that matter? He had nowhere to go. Those who had pursued him must have realized that. Without a horse he could not cross back to Pikarayd, the most easterly of the Young Kingdoms. Without a boat he could not venture onto that sea and try to steer a course back to the Isle of the Purple Towns. He recalled no map which showed an eastern sea and he had little idea of how far he had traveled from Pikarayd. He decided that his only hope of surviving was to go north, following the coast in the trust that sooner or later he would come upon a port or a fishing village where he might trade his few remaining belongings for a passage on a boat. Yet that hope was a small one, for his food and his drugs could hardly last more than a day or so.

He took a deep breath to steel himself for the march and then regretted it; the mist cut at his throat and his lungs like a thousand tiny knives. He coughed. He spat upon the shingle.

And he heard something, something other than the moody whisperings of the sea: a regular creaking sound, as of a man walking in stiff leather. His right hand went to his left hip and the sword which rested there. He turned about, peering in every direction for the source of the noise, but the mist distorted it. It could have come from anywhere.

Elric crept back to the rock where he had sheltered. He leaned against it so that no swordsman could take him unawares from behind. He waited.

The creaking came again, but other sounds were added. He heard a clanking; a splash; perhaps a voice, perhaps a footfall on timber; and he guessed that either he was experiencing a hallucination as a side effect of the drug he had just swallowed or he had heard a ship coming toward the beach and dropping its anchor.

He felt relieved and he was tempted to laugh at himself for assuming so readily that this coast must be uninhabited. He had thought that the bleak cliffs stretched for miles—perhaps hundreds of miles—in all directions. The assumption could easily have been the subjective result of his depression, his weariness. It occurred to him that he might as easily have discovered a land not shown on maps, yet with a sophisticated culture of its own: with sailing ships, for instance, and harbors for them. Yet still he did not reveal himself.

Instead he withdrew behind the rock, peering into the mist toward the sea. And at last he discerned a shadow which had not been there the previous night. A black, angular shadow which could only be a ship. He made out the suggestion of ropes, he heard men grunting, he heard the creak and the rasp of a yard as it traveled up a mast. The sail was being furled.

Elric waited at least an hour, expecting the crew of the ship to disembark. They could have no other reason for entering this treacherous bay. But a silence had descended, as if the whole ship slept.

Cautiously Elric emerged from behind the rock and

walked down to the edge of the sea. Now he could see
the ship a little more clearly. Red sunlight was behind it,
thin and watery, diffused by the mist. It was a good-
sized ship and fashioned throughout of the same dark
wood. Its design was baroque and unfamiliar, with high
decks fore and aft and no evidence of rowing ports.
This was unusual in a ship either of Melnibonéan or
Young Kingdoms design and it tended to prove his
theory that he had stumbled upon a civilization for some
reason cut off from the rest of the world, just as Elwher
and the Unmapped Kingdoms were cut off by the vast
stretches of the Sighing Desert and the Weeping Waste.
He saw no movement aboard, heard none of the sounds
one might usually expect to hear on a seagoing ship, even
if the larger part of the crew was resting. The mist eddied
and more of the red light poured through to illuminate
the vessel, revealing the large wheels on both the foredeck and the reardeck, the slender mast with its furled
sail, the complicated geometrical carvings of its rails
and its figurehead, the great, curving prow which gave
the ship its main impression of power and strength and
made Elric think it must be a warship rather than a trading vessel. But who was there to fight in such waters as
these?

He cast aside his wariness and cupped his hands about
his mouth, calling out:

"Hail, the ship!"

The answering silence seemed to him to take on a peculiar hesitancy as if those on board heard him and
wondered if they should answer.

"Hail, the ship!"

Then a figure appeared on the port rail and, leaning
over, looked casually toward him. The figure had on
armor as dark and as strange as the design of his ship; he
had a helmet obscuring most of his face and the main
feature that Elric could distinguish was a thick, golden
beard and sharp blue eyes.

"Hail, the shore," said the armored man. His accent
was unknown to Elric, his tone was as casual as his manner. Elric thought he smiled. "What do you seek with us?"

"Aid," said Elric. "I am stranded here. My horse is dead. I am lost."

"Lost? Aha!" The man's voice echoed in the mist. "Lost. And you wish to come aboard?"

"I can pay a little. I can give my services in return for a passage, either to your next port of call or to some land close to the Young Kingdoms where maps are available so that I could make my own way thereafter. . . ."

"Well," said the other slowly, "there's work for a swordsman."

"I have a sword," said Elric.

"I see it. A good, big battle-blade."

"Then I can come aboard?"

"We must confer first. If you would be good enough to wait awhile . . ."

"Of course," said Elric. He was nonplussed by the man's manner, but the prospect of warmth and food on board the ship was cheering. He waited patiently until the blond-bearded warrior came back to the rail.

"Your name, sir?" said the warrior.

"I am Elric of Melniboné."

The warrior seemed to be consulting a parchment, running his finger down a list until he nodded, satisfied, and put the list into his large-buckled belt.

"Well," he said, "there was some point in waiting here, after all. I found it difficult to believe."

"What was the dispute and why did you wait?"

"For you," said the warrior, heaving a rope ladder over the side so that its end fell into the sea. "Will you board now, Elric of Melniboné?"

Elric was surprised by how shallow the water was and he wondered by what means such a large vessel could come so close to the shore. Shoulder-deep in the sea he reached up to grasp the ebony rungs of the ladder. He

had great difficulty heaving himself from the water and
was further hampered by the swaying of the ship and
the weight of his runesword, but eventually he had
clambered awkwardly over the side and stood on the
deck with the water running from his clothes to the timbers and his body shivering with cold. He looked about
him. Shining, red-tinted mist clung about the ship's dark
yards and rigging, white mist spread itself over the roofs
and sides of the two large cabins set fore and aft of the
mast, and this mist was not of the same character as the
mist beyond the ship. Elric, for a moment, had the fanci-
ful notion that the mist traveled permanently wherever
the ship traveled. He smiled to himself, putting the
dreamlike quality of his experience down to lack of food
and sleep. When the ship sailed into sunnier waters he
would see it for the relatively ordinary vessel it was.

The blond warrior took Elric's arm. The man was as
tall as Elric and massively built. Within his helm he
smiled, saying:

"Let us go below."

They went to the cabin forward of the mast and the
warrior drew back a sliding door, standing aside to let
Elric enter first. Elric ducked his head and went into the
warmth of the cabin. A lamp of red-gray glass gleamed,
hanging from four silver chains attached to the roof,
revealing several more bulky figures, fully dressed in a
variety of armors, seated about a square and sturdy
sea-table. All faces turned to regard Elric as he came in,
followed by the blond warrior who said:

"This is he."

One of the occupants of the cabin, who sat in the far-
thest corner and whose features were completely hidden
by the shadow, nodded. "Aye," he said. "That is he."

"You know me, sir," said Elric, seating himself at the
end of the bench and removing his sodden leather cloak.
The warrior nearest him passed him a metal cup of hot
wine and Elric accepted it gratefully, sipping at the spiced
liquid and marveling at how quickly it dispersed the
chill within him.

"In a sense," said the man in the shadows. His voice

was sardonic and at the same time had a melancholy ring, and Elric was not offended, for the bitterness in the voice seemed directed more at the owner than at any he addressed.

The blond warrior seated himself opposite Elric. "I am Brut," he said, "once of Lashmar, where my family still holds land, but it is many a year since I have been there."

"From the Young Kingdoms, then?" said Elric.

"Aye. Once."

"This ship journeys nowhere near those nations?" Elric asked.

"I believe it does not," said Brut. "It is not so long, I think, since I myself came aboard. I was seeking Tanelorn, but found this craft, instead."

"Tanelorn?" Elric smiled. "How many must seek that mythical place? Do you know of one called Rackhir, once a warrior priest of Phum? We adventured together quite recently. He left to look for Tanelorn."

"I do not know him," said Brut of Lashmar.

"And these waters," said Elric, "do they lie far from the Young Kingdoms?"

"Very far," said the man in the shadows.

"Are you from Elwher, perhaps?" asked Elric. "Or from any other of what we in the west call the Unmapped Kingdoms?"

"Most of our lands are not on your maps," said the man in the shadows. And he laughed. Again Elric found that he was not offended. And he was not particularly troubled by the mysteries hinted at by the man in the shadows. Soldiers of fortune (as he deemed these men to be) were fond of their private jokes and references; it was usually all that united them save a common willingness to hire their swords to whomever could pay.

Outside the anchor was rattling and the ship rolled. Elric heard the yard being lowered and he heard the smack of the sail as it was unfurled. He wondered how they hoped to leave the bay with so little wind available. He noticed that the faces of the other warriors (where their faces were visible) had taken on a rather set look as the ship began to move. He looked from one grim, haunted face to another and he wondered if his own features bore the same cast.

"For where do we sail?" he asked.

Brut shrugged. "I know only that we had to stop to wait for you, Elric of Melniboné."

"You knew I would be there?"

The man in the shadows stirred and helped himself to more hot wine from the jug set into a hole in the center of the table. "You are the last one we need," he said. "I was the first taken aboard. So far I have not regretted my decision to make the voyage."

"Your name, sir?" Elric decided he would no longer be at that particular disadvantage.

"Oh, names? Names? I have so many. The one I favor is Erekosë. But I have been called Urlik Skarsol and John Daker and Ilian of Garathorm to my certain knowledge. Some would have me believe that I have been Elric Womanslayer. . . ."

"Womanslayer? An unpleasant nickname. Who is this other Elric?"

"That I cannot completely answer," said Erekosë. "But I share a name, it seems, with more than one aboard this ship. I, like Brut, sought Tanelorn and found myself here instead."

"We have that in common," said another. He was a black-skinned warrior, the tallest of the company, his features oddly enhanced by a scar running like an inverted V from his forehead and over both eyes, down his cheeks to his jawbones. "I was in a land called Ghaja-Ki, a most unpleasant, swampy place, filled with perverse and diseased life. I had heard of a city said to exist there and I thought it might be Tanelorn. It was not. And it was inhabited by a blue-skinned, hermaphroditic race who determined to cure me of what they considered my malformations of hue and sexuality. This scar you see was their work. The pain of their operation gave me strength to escape them and I ran naked into the swamps, floundering for many a mile until the swamp became a lake feeding a broad river over which hung black clouds of insects which set upon me hungrily. This ship appeared and I was more than glad to seek its sanctuary. I am Otto Blendker, once a scholar of Brunse, now a hireling sword for my sins."

"This Brunse? Does it lie near Elwher?" said Elric. He had never heard of such a place, nor such an outlandish name, in the Young Kingdoms.

The black man shook his head. "I know naught of El-wher."

"Then the world is a considerably larger place than I imagined," said Elric.

"Indeed it is," said Erekosë. "What would you say if I offered you the theory that the sea on which we sail spans more than one world?"

"I would be inclined to believe you." Elric smiled. "I have studied such theories. More, I have experienced adventures in worlds other than my own."

"It is a relief to hear it," said Erekosë. "Not all on board this ship are willing to accept my theory."

"I come closer to accepting it," said Otto Blendker, "though I find it terrifying."

"It is that," agreed Erekosë. "More terrifying than you can imagine, friend Otto."

Elric leaned across the table and helped himself to a further mug of wine. His clothes were already drying and physically he had a sense of well-being. "I'll be glad to leave this misty shore behind."

"The shore has been left already," said Brut, "but as for the mist, it is ever with us. Mist appears to follow the ship—or else the ship creates the mist wherever it travels. It is rare that we see land at all and when we do see it, as we saw it today, it is usually obscured, like a reflection in a dull and buckled shield."

"We sail on a supernatural sea," said another, holding out a gloved hand for the jug. Elric passed it to him. "In Hasghan, where I come from, we have a legend of a Bewitched Sea. If a mariner finds himself sailing in those waters he may never return and will be lost for eternity."

"Your legend contains at least some truth, I fear, Terndrik of Hasghan," Brut said.

"How many warriors are on board?" Elric asked.

"Sixteen other than the Four," said Erekosë. "Twenty in all. The crew numbers about ten and then there is the captain. You will see him soon, doubtless."

"The Four? Who are they?"

Erekosë laughed. "You and I are two of them. The other two occupy the aft cabin. And if you wish to know *why* we are called the Four, you must ask the captain, though I warn you his answers are rarely satisfying."

Elric realized that he was being pressed slightly to one side. "The ship makes good speed," he said laconically, "considering how poor the wind was."

"Excellent speed," agreed Erekosë. He rose from his corner, a broad-shouldered man with an ageless face bearing the evidence of considerable experience. He was handsome and he had plainly seen much conflict, for both his hands and his face were heavily scarred, though not disfigured. His eyes, though deep-set and dark, seemed of no particular color and yet were familiar to Elric. He felt that he might have seen those eyes in a dream once.

"Have we met before?" Elric asked him.

"Oh, possibly—or shall meet. What does it matter? Our fates are the same. We share an identical doom. And possibly we share more than that."

"More? I hardly comprehend the first part of your statement."

"Then it is for the best," said Erekosë, inching past his comrades and emerging on the other side of the table. He laid a surprisingly gentle hand on Elric's shoulder. "Come, we must seek audience with the captain. He expressed a wish to see you shortly after you came aboard."

Elric nodded and rose. "This captain—what is his name?"

"He has none he will reveal to us," said Erekosë. Together they emerged onto the deck. The mist was if anything thicker and of the same deathly whiteness, no longer

tinted by the sun's rays. It was hard to see to the far
ends of the ship and for all that they were evidently
moving rapidly, there was no hint of a wind. Yet it was
warmer than Elric might have expected. He followed
Erekosë forward to the cabin set under the deck on which
one of the ship's twin wheels stood, tended by a tall
man in sea-coat and leggings of quilted deerskin who was
so still as to resemble a statue. The red-haired steersman
did not look around or down as they advanced toward
the cabin, but Elric caught a glimpse of his face.

The door seemed built of some kind of smooth metal
possessing a sheen almost like the healthy coat of an
animal. It was reddish-brown and the most colorful
thing Elric had so far seen on the ship. Erekosë knocked
softly upon the door. "Captain," he said. "Elric is here."

"Enter," said a voice at once melodious and distant.

The door opened. Rosy light flooded out, half-blind-
ing Elric as he walked in. As his eyes adapted, he could
see a very tall, pale-clad man standing upon a richly hued
carpet in the middle of the cabin. Elric heard the door
close and realized that Erekosë had not accompanied him
inside.

"Are you refreshed, Elric?" said the captain.

"I am, sir, thanks to your wine."

The captain's features were no more human than were
Elric's. They were at once finer and more powerful than
those of the Melnibonéan, yet bore a slight resemblance
in that the eyes were inclined to taper, as did the face,
toward the chin. The captain's long hair fell to his
shoulders in red-gold waves and was kept back from his
brow by a circlet of blue jade. His body was clad in
buff-colored tunic and hose and there were sandals of
silver and silver-thread laced to his calves. Apart from
his clothing, he was twin to the steersman Elric had recently seen.

"Will you have more wine?"

The captain moved toward a chest on the far side of
the cabin, near the porthole, which was closed.

"Thank you," said Elric. And now he realized why
the eyes had not focused on him. The captain was blind.

For all that his movements were deft and assured, it was obvious that he could not see at all. He poured the wine from a silver jug into a silver cup and began to cross toward Elric, holding the cup out before him. Elric stepped forward and accepted it.

"I am grateful for your decision to join us," said the captain. "I am much relieved, sir."

"You are courteous," said Elric, "though I must add that my decision was not difficult to make. I had nowhere else to go."

"I understand that. It is why we put into shore when and where we did. You will find that all your companions were in a similar position before they, too, came aboard."

"You appear to have considerable knowledge of the movements of many men," said Elric. He held the wine untasted in his left hand.

"Many," agreed the captain, "on many worlds. I understand that you are a person of culture, sir, so you will be aware of something of the nature of the sea upon which my ship sails."

"I think so."

"She sails between the worlds, for the most part—between the planes of a variety of aspects of the same world, to be a little more exact." The captain hesitated, turning his blind face away from Elric. "Please know that I do not deliberately mystify you. There are some things I do not understand and other things which I may not completely reveal. It is a trust I have and I hope you feel you can respect it."

"I have no reason as yet to do otherwise," replied the albino. And he took a sip of the wine.

"I find myself with a fine company," said the captain. "I hope that you continue to think it worthwhile honoring my trust when we reach our destination."

"And what is that, Captain?"

"An island indigenous to these waters."

"That must be a rarity."

"Indeed, it is, and once undiscovered, uninhabited by those we must count our enemies. Now that they have found it and realize its power, we are in great danger."

"We? You mean your race or those aboard your ship?"

The captain smiled. "I have no race, save myself. I speak, I suppose, of all humanity."

"These enemies are not human, then?"

"No. They are inextricably involved in human affairs, but this fact has not instilled in them any loyalty to us. I use 'humanity,' of course, in its broader sense, to include yourself and myself."

"I understood," said Elric. "What is this folk called?"

"Many things," said the captain. "Forgive me, but I cannot continue longer now. If you will ready yourself for battle I assure you that I will reveal more to you as soon as the time is right."

Only when Elric stood again outside the reddish-brown door, watching Erekosë advancing up the deck through the mist, did the albino wonder if the captain had charmed him to the point where he had forgotten all common sense. Yet the blind man had impressed him and he had, after all, nothing better to do than to sail on to the island. He shrugged. He could always alter his decision if he discovered that those upon the island were not, in his opinion, enemies.

"Are you more mystified or less, Elric?" said Erekosë, smiling.

"More mystified in some ways, less in others," Elric told him. "And, for some reason, I do not care."

"Then you share the feeling of the whole company," Erekosë told him.

It was only when Erekosë led him to the cabin aft of the mast that Elric realized he had not asked the captain what the significance of the Four might be.

Save that it faced in the opposite direction, the other cabin resembled the first in almost every detail. Here,

too, were seated some dozen men, all experienced soldiers of fortune by their features and their clothing.
Two sat together at the center of the table's starboard
side. One was bareheaded, fair, and careworn, the other
had features resembling Elric's own and he seemed to
be wearing a silver gauntlet on his left hand while the
right hand was naked; his armor was delicate and outlandish. He looked up as Elric entered and there was
recognition in his single eye (the other was covered by a
brocade-work patch).

"Elric of Melniboné!" he exclaimed. "My theories become more meaningful!" He turned to his companion.
"See, Hawkmoon, this is the one of whom I spoke."

"You know me, sir?" Elric was nonplussed.

"You recognize me, Elric. You must! At the Tower
of Voilodion Ghagnasdiak? With Erekosë—though a different Erekosë."

"I know of no such tower, no name which resembles
that, and this is the first I have seen of Erekosë. You know
me and you know my name, but I do not know you. I find
this disconcerting, sir."

"I, too, had never met Prince Corum before he came
aboard," said Erekosë, "yet he insists we fought together
once. I am inclined to believe him. Time on the different
planes does not always run concurrently. Prince Corum
might well exist in what we would term the future."

"I had thought to find some relief from such paradoxes
here," said Hawkmoon, passing his hand over his face.
He smiled bleakly. "But it seems there is none at this
present moment in the history of the planes. Everything
is in flux and even our identities, it seems, are prone to
alter at any moment."

"We were Three," said Corum. "Do you not recall it,
Elric? The Three Who Are One?"

Elric shook his head.

Corum shrugged, saying softly to himself, "Well,
now we are Four. Did the captain say anything of an island we are supposed to invade?"

"He did," said Elric. "Do you know who these enemies
might be?"

"We know no more or less than do you, Elric," said Hawkmoon. "I seek a place called Tanelorn and two children. Perhaps I seek the Runestaff, too. Of that I am not entirely sure."

"We found it once," said Corum. "We three. In the Tower of Voilodion Ghagnasdiak. It was of considerable help to us."

"As it might be to me," Hawkmoon told him. "I served it once. I gave it a great deal."

"We have much in common," Erekosë put in, "as I told you, Elric. Perhaps we share masters in common, too?"

Elric shrugged. "I serve no master but myself."

And he wondered why they all smiled in the same strange way.

Erekosë said quietly, "On such ventures as these one is inclined to forget much, as one forgets a dream."

"This *is* a dream," said Hawkmoon. "Of late I've dreamed many such."

"It is all dreaming, if you like," said Corum. "All existence."

Elric was not interested in such philosophizing. "Dream or reality, the experience amounts to the same, does it not?"

"Quite right," said Erekosë with a wan smile.

They talked on for another hour or two until Corum stretched and yawned and commented that he was feeling sleepy. The others agreed that they were all tired and so they left the cabin and went aft and below where there were bunks for all the warriors. As he stretched himself out in one of the bunks, Elric said to Brut of Lashmar, who had climbed into the bunk above:

"It would help to know when this fight begins."

Brut looked over the edge, down at the prone albino. "I think it will be soon," he said.

Elric stood alone upon the deck, leaning upon the rail and trying to make out the sea, but the sea, like the rest of the world, was hidden by white curling mist. Elric wondered if there were waters flowing under the ship's keel at all. He looked up to where the sail was tight and swollen at the mast, filled with a warm and powerful wind. It was light, but again it was not possible to tell the hour of the day. Puzzled by Corum's comments concerning an earlier meeting, Elric wondered if there had been other dreams in his life such as this might be—dreams he had forgotten completely upon awakening. But the uselessness of such speculation became quickly evident and he turned his attention to more immediate matters, wondering at the origin of the captain and his strange ship sailing on a stranger ocean.

"The captain," said Hawkmoon's voice, and Elric turned to bid good morning to the tall, fair-haired man who bore a strange, regular scar in the center of his forehead, "has requested that we four visit him in his cabin."

The other two emerged from the mist and together they made their way to the prow, knocking on the reddish-brown door and being at once admitted into the presence of the blind captain, who had four silver wine-cups already poured for them. He gestured them toward the great chest on which the wine stood. "Please help yourselves, my friends."

They did so, standing there with the cups in their hands, four tall, doom-haunted swordsmen, each of a strikingly different cast of features, yet each bearing a certain stamp which marked them as being of a like kind. Elric noticed it, for all that he was one of them, and he tried to recall the details of what Corum had told him on the previous evening.

"We are nearing our destination," said the captain. "It will not be long before we disembark. I do not believe our enemies expect us, yet it will be a hard fight against those two."

"Two?" said Hawkmoon. "Only two?"

"Only two." The captain smiled. "A brother and a sister. Sorcerers from quite another universe than ours. Due to recent disruptions in the fabric of our worlds— of which you know something, Hawkmoon, and you, too, Corum—certain beings have been released who

would not otherwise have the power they now possess.
And possessing great power, they crave for more—
for all the power that there is in our universe. These
beings are amoral in a way in which the Lords of Law
or Chaos are not. They do not fight for influence upon
the Earth, as those gods do; their only wish is to convert
the essential energy of our universe to their own uses. I
believe they foster some ambition in their particular universe which would be furthered if they could achieve
their wish. At present, in spite of conditions highly favor-
able to them, they have not attained their full strength,
but the time is not far off before they do attain it. Agak
and Gagak is how they are called in human tongue and
they are outside the power of any of our gods, so a more
powerful group has been summoned—yourselves. The
Champion Eternal in four of his incarnations (and four
is the maximum number we can risk without precipitating further unwelcome disruptions among the planes of
Earth)—Erekosë, Elric, Corum, and Hawkmoon. Each
of you will command four others, whose fates are linked
with your own and who are great fighters in their own
right, though they do not share your destinies in every
sense. You may each pick the four with whom you wish
to fight. I think you will find it easy enough to decide.
We make landfall quite shortly now."

"You will lead us?" Hawkmoon said.

"I cannot. I can only take you to the island and wait for
those who survive—if any survive."

Elric frowned. "This fight is not mine, I think."

"It is yours," said the captain soberly. "And it is mine.
I would land with you if that were permitted me, but it
is not."

"Why so?" asked Corum.

"You will learn that one day. I have not the courage to
tell you. I bear you nothing but goodwill, however. Be
assured of that."

Erekosë rubbed his jaw. "Well, since it is my destiny
to fight, and since I, like Hawkmoon, continue to seek
Tanelorn, and since I gather there is some chance of my

fulfilling my ambition if I am successful, I for one agree to go against these two, Agak and Gagak."

Hawkmoon nodded. "I go with Erekosë, for similar reasons."

"And I," said Corum.

"Not long since," said Elric, "I counted myself without comrades. Now I have many. For that reason alone I will fight with them."

"It is perhaps the best of reasons," said Erekosë approvingly.

"There is no reward for this work, save my assurance that your success will save the world much misery," said the captain. "And for you, Elric, there is less reward than the rest may hope for."

"Perhaps not," said Elric.

"As you say." The captain gestured toward the jug of wine. "More wine, my friends?"

They each accepted, while the captain continued, his blind face staring upward at the roof of the cabin.

"Upon this island is a ruin—perhaps it was once a city called Tanelorn—and at the center of the ruin stands one whole building. It is this building which Agak and his sister use. It is that which you must attack. You will recognize it, I hope, at once."

"And we must slay this pair?" said Erekosë.

"If you can. They have servants who help them. These must be slain, also. Then the building must be fired. This is important." The captain paused. "Fired. It must be destroyed in no other way."

Elric smiled a dry smile. "There are few other ways of destroying buildings, Sir Captain."

The captain returned his smile and made a slight bow of acknowledgment. "Aye, it's so. Nonetheless, it is worth remembering what I have said."

"Do you know what these two look like, these Agak and Gagak?" Corum asked.

"No. It is possible that they resemble creatures of our own worlds; it is possible that they do not. Few have seen them. It is only recently that they have been able to materialize at all."

"And how may they best be overwhelmed?" asked
Hawkmoon.

"By courage and ingenuity," said the captain.

"You are not very explicit, sir," said Elric.

"I am as explicit as I can be. Now, my friends, I suggest
you rest and prepare your arms."

As they returned to their cabins, Erekosë sighed.

"We are fated," he said. "We have little free will, for
all we deceive ourselves otherwise. If we perish or live
through this venture, it will not count for much in the
overall scheme of things."

"I think you are of a gloomy turn of mind, friend,"
said Hawkmoon.

The mist snaked through the branches of the mast,
writhing in the rigging, flooding the deck. It swirled
across the faces of the other three men as Elric looked
at them.

"A realistic turn of mind," said Corum.

The mist massed more thickly upon the deck, mantling
each man like a shroud. The timbers of the ship creaked
and to Elric's ears took on the sound of a raven's croak.
It was colder now. In silence they went to their cabins to
test the hooks and buckles of their armor, to polish and
to sharpen their weapons and to pretend to sleep.

"Oh, I've no liking for sorcery," said Brut of Lashmar, tugging at his golden beard, "for sorcery it was
resulted in my shame." Elric had told him all that the
captain had said and had asked Brut to be one of the
four who fought with him when they landed.

"It is all sorcery here," Otto Blendker said. And he
smiled wanly as he gave Elric his hand. "I'll fight beside
you, Elric."

His sea-green armor shimmering faintly in the lantern
light, another rose, his casque pushed back from his face.
It was a face almost as white as Elric's, though the
eyes were deep and near-black. "And I," said Hown Serpent-tamer, "though I fear I'm little use on still land."

The last to rise, at Elric's glance, was a warrior who
had said little during their earlier conversations. His

voice was deep and hesitant. He wore a plain iron battle-cap and the red hair beneath it was braided. At the end of each braid was a small fingerbone which rattled on the shoulders of his byrnie as he moved. This was Ashnar the Lynx, whose eyes were rarely less than fierce. "I lack the eloquence or the breeding of you other gentlemen," said Ashnar. "And I've no familiarity with sorcery or those other things of which you speak, but I'm a good soldier and my joy is in fighting. I'll take your orders, Elric, if you'll have me."

"Willingly," said Elric.

"There is no dispute, it seems," said Erekosë to the remaining four who had elected to join him. "All this is doubtless preordained. Our destinies have been linked from the first."

"Such philosophy can lead to unhealthy fatalism," said Terndrik of Hasghan. "Best believe our fates are our own, even if the evidence denies it."

"You must think as you wish," said Erekosë. "I have led many lives, though all, save one, are remembered but faintly." He shrugged. "Yet I deceive myself, I suppose, in that I work for a time when I shall find this Tanelorn and perhaps be reunited with the one I seek. That ambition is what gives me energy, Terndrik."

Elric smiled. "I fight, I think, because I relish the comradeship of battle. That, in itself, is a melancholy condition in which to find oneself, is it not?"

"Aye." Erekosë glanced at the floor. "Well, we must try to rest now."

IV

The outlines of the coast were dim. They waded through white water and white mist, their swords held above their heads. Swords were their only weapons. Each of the Four possessed a blade of unusual size and design, but none bore a sword which occasionally murmured to

itself as did Elric's Stormbringer. Glancing back, Elric
saw the captain standing at the rail, his blind face
turned toward the island, his pale lips moving as if he
spoke to himself. Now the water was waist-deep and the
sand beneath Elric's feet hardened and became smooth
rock. He waded on, wary and ready to carry any attack to those who might be defending the island. But
now the mist grew thinner, as if it could gain no hold on
the land, and there were no obvious signs of defenders.

Tucked into his belt, each man had a brand, its end
wrapped in oiled cloth so that it should not be wet when
the time came to light it. Similarly, each was equipped
with a handful of smoldering tinder in a little firebox in
a pouch attached to his belt, so that the brands could
be instantly ignited.

"Only fire will destroy this enemy forever," the captain had said again as he handed them their brands and
their tinderboxes.

As the mist cleared, it revealed a landscape of dense
shadows. The shadows spread over red rock and yellow
vegetation and they were shadows of all shapes and
dimensions, resembling all manner of things. They
seemed cast by the huge blood-colored sun which stood
at perpetual noon above the island, but what was disturbing about them was that the shadows themselves seemed
without a source, as if the objects they represented were
invisible or existed elsewhere than on the island itself. The sky, too, seemed full of these shadows, but
whereas those on the island were still, those in the sky
sometimes moved, perhaps when the clouds moved. And
all the while the red sun poured down its bloody light and
touched the twenty men with its unwelcome radiance
just as it touched the land.

And at times, as they advanced cautiously inland, a
peculiar flickering light sometimes crossed the island so
that the outlines of the place became unsteady for a few
seconds before returning to focus. Elric suspected his
eyes and said nothing until Hown Serpent-tamer (who
was having difficulty finding his land-legs) remarked:

"I have rarely been ashore, it's true, but I think the

quality of this land is stranger than any other I've known. It shimmers. It distorts."

Several voices agreed with him.

"And from whence come all these shadows?" Ashnar the Lynx stared around him in unashamed superstitious awe. "Why cannot we see that which casts them?"

"It could be," Corum said, "that these are shadows cast by objects existing in other dimensions of the Earth. If all dimensions meet here, as has been suggested, that could be a likely explanation." He put his silver hand to his embroidered eye-patch. "This is not the strangest example I have witnessed of such a conjunction."

"Likely?" Otto Blendker snorted. "Pray let none give me an *unlikely* explanation, if you please!"

They pressed on through the shadows and the lurid light until they arrived at the outskirts of the ruins.

These ruins, thought Elric, had something in common with the ramshackle city of Ameeron, which he had visited on his quest for the Black Sword. But they were altogether more vast—more a collection of smaller cities, each one in a radically different architectural style.

"Perhaps this is Tanelorn," said Corum, who had visited the place, "or, rather, all the versions of Tanelorn there have ever been. For Tanelorn exists in many forms, each form depending upon the wishes of those who most desire to find her."

"This is not the Tanelorn I expected to find," said Hawkmoon bitterly.

"Nor I," added Erekosë bleakly.

"Perhaps it is not Tanelorn," said Elric. "Perhaps it is not."

"Or perhaps this is a graveyard," said Corum distantly, frowning with his single eye. "A graveyard containing all the forgotten versions of that strange city."

They began to clamber over the ruins, their arms clattering as they moved, heading for the center of the place. Elric could tell by the introspective expressions in the faces of many of his companions that they, like him, were wondering if this were not a dream. Why else should they find themselves in this peculiar situation, unques-

tioningly risking their lives—perhaps their souls—in a
fight with which none of them was identified?

Erekosë moved closer to Elric as they marched. "Have
you noticed," said he, "that the shadows now represent
something?"

Elric nodded. "You can tell from the ruins what some
of the buildings looked like when they were whole. The
shadows are the shadows of those buildings—the original
buildings before they became ruined."

"Just so," said Erekosë. Together, they shuddered.

At last they approached the likely center of the place
and here was a building which was not ruined. It
stood in a cleared space, all curves and ribbons of metal
and glowing tubes.

"It resembles a machine more than a building," said
Hawkmoon.

"And a musical instrument more than a machine,"
Corum mused.

The party came to a halt, each group of four gathering about its leader. There was no question but that they
had arrived at their goal.

Now that Elric looked carefully at the building he
could see that it was in fact two buildings—both abso-
lutely identical and joined at various points by curling
systems of pipes which might be connecting corridors,
though it was difficult to imagine what manner of being
could utilize them.

"Two buildings," said Erekosë. "We were not prepared
for this. Shall we split up and attack both?"

Instinctively Elric felt that this action would be unwise. He shook his head. "I think we should go together
into one, else our strength will be weakened."

"I agree," said Hawkmoon, and the rest nodded.

Thus, there being no cover to speak of, they marched
boldly toward the nearest building to a point near the
ground where a black opening of irregular proportions
could be discerned. Ominously, there was still no sign
of defenders. The buildings pulsed and glowed and occasionally whispered, but that was all.

Elric and his party were the first to enter, finding themselves in a damp, warm passage which curved almost immediately to the right. They were followed by the others until all stood in this passage warily glaring ahead, expecting to be attacked. But no attack came.

With Elric at their head, they moved on for some moments before the passage began to tremble violently and sent Hown Serpent-tamer crashing to the floor cursing. As the man in the sea-green armor scrambled up, a voice began to echo along the passage, seemingly coming from a great distance yet nonetheless loud and irritable.

"Who? Who? Who?" shrieked the voice.

"Who? Who? Who invades me?"

The passage's tremble susbsided a little into a constant quivering motion. The voice became a muttering, detached and uncertain.

"What attacks? What?"

The twenty men glanced at one another in puzzlement. At length Elric shrugged and led the party on and soon the passage had widened out into a hall whose walls, roof, and floor were damp with sticky fluid and whose air was hard to breathe. And now, somehow passing themselves through the walls of this hall, came the first of the defenders, ugly beasts who must be the servants of that mysterious brother and sister Agak and Gagak.

"Attack!" cried the distant voice. *"Destroy this. Destroy it!"*

The beasts were of a primitive sort, mostly gaping mouth and slithering body, but there were many of them oozing toward the twenty men, who quickly formed themselves into the four fighting units and prepared to defend themselves. The creatures made a dreadful slushing sound as they approached and the ridges of bone which served them as teeth clashed as they reared up to snap at Elric and his companions. Elric whirled his sword and it met hardly any resistance as it sliced through several of the things at once. But now the air was thicker than ever and a stench threatened to overwhelm them as fluid drenched the floor.

"Move on through them," Elric instructed, "hacking a

path through as you go. Head for yonder opening." He
pointed with his left hand.

And so they advanced, cutting back hundreds of the
primitive beasts and thus decreasing the breathability of
the air.

"The creatures are not hard to fight," gasped Hown
Serpent-tamer, "but each one we kill robs us a little of
our own chances of life."

Elric was aware of the irony. "Cunningly planned
by our enemies, no doubt." He coughed and slashed
again at a dozen of the beasts slithering toward him.
The things were fearless, but they were stupid, too. They
made no attempt at strategy.

Finally Elric reached the next passage, where the air
was slightly purer. He sucked gratefully at the sweeter
atmosphere and waved his companions on.

Sword-arms rising and falling, they gradually retreated
back into the passage, followed by only a few of the beasts.
The creatures seemed reluctant to enter the passage and
Elric suspected that somewhere within it there must lie a
danger which even they feared. There was nothing for
it, however, but to press on and he was only grateful
that all twenty had survived this initial ordeal.

Gasping, they rested for a moment, leaning against
the trembling walls of the passage, listening to the tones
of that distant voice, now muffled and indistinct.

"I like not this castle at all," growled Brut of Lashmar, inspecting a rent in his cloak where a creature had
seized it. "High sorcery commands it."

"It is only what we knew," Ashnar the Lynx reminded
him, and Ashnar was plainly hard put to control his
terror. The fingerbones in his braids kept time with the
trembling of the walls and the huge barbarian looked
almost pathetic as he steeled himself to go on.

"They are cowards, these sorcerers," Otto Blendker
said. "They do not show themselves." He raised his
voice. "Is their aspect so loathsome that they are afraid
lest we look upon them?" It was a challenge not taken
up. As they pushed on through the passages there was
no sign either of Agak or his sister Gagak. It became

gloomier and brighter in turns. Sometimes the passages
narrowed so that it was difficult to squeeze their bodies
through, sometimes they widened into what were almost
halls. Most of the time they appeared to be climbing
higher into the building.

Elric tried to guess the nature of the building's inhabitants. There were no steps in the castle, no artifacts he
could recognize. For no particular reason he developed an
image of Agak and Gagak as reptilian in form, for reptiles would prefer gently rising passages to steps and
doubtless would have little need of conventional furni-
ture. There again it was possible that they could change
their shape at will, assuming human form when it suited
them. He was becoming impatient to face either one or
both of the sorcerers.

Ashnar the Lynx had other reasons—or so he said—
for his own lack of patience.

"They said there'd be treasure here," he muttered. "I
thought to stake my life against a fair reward, but
there's naught here of value." He put a horny hand
against the damp material of the wall. "Not even stone or
brick. What are these walls made of, Elric?"

Elric shook his head. "That has puzzled me, also,
Ashnar."

Then Elric saw large, fierce eyes peering out of the
gloom ahead. He heard a rattling noise, a rushing noise,
and the eyes grew larger and larger. He saw a red
mouth, yellow fangs, orange fur. Then the growling
sounded and the beast sprang at him even as he raised
Stormbringer to defend himself and shouted a warning to
the others. The creature was a baboon, but huge, and
there were at least a dozen others following the first. Elric drove his body forward behind his sword, taking
the beast in its groin. Claws reached out and dug into his
shoulders and waist. He groaned as he felt at least one
set of claws draw blood. His arms were trapped and he
could not pull Stormbringer free. All he could do was
twist the sword in the wound he had already made. With
all his might, he turned the hilt. The great ape shouted,
its bloodshot eyes blazing, and it bared its yellow fangs

as its muzzle shot toward Elric's throat. The teeth closed
on his neck, the stinking breath threatened to choke
him. Again he twisted the blade. Again the beast yelled
in pain.

The fangs were pressing into the metal of Elric's gor-
get, the only thing saving him from immediate death. He
struggled to free at least one arm, twisting the sword for
the third time, then tugging it sideways to widen the
wound in the groin. The growls and groans of the baboon grew more intense and the teeth tightened their hold
on his neck, but now, mingled with the noises of the ape,
he began to hear a murmuring and he felt Stormbringer
pulse in his hand. He knew that the sword was drawing
power from the ape even as the ape sought to destroy
him. Some of that power began to flow into his body.

Desperately Elric put all his remaining strength into
dragging the sword across the ape's body, slitting its belly
wide so that its blood and entrails spilled over him as he
was suddenly free and staggering backward, wrenching the
sword out in the same movement. The ape, too, was staggering back, staring down in stupefied awe at its own
horrible wound before it fell to the floor of the passage.

Elric turned, ready to give aid to his nearest comrade, and he was in time to see Terndrik of Hasghan
die, kicking in the clutches of an even larger ape, his
head bitten clean from his shoulders and his red blood
gouting.

Elric drove Stormbringer cleanly between the shoulders of Terndrik's slayer, taking the ape in the heart.
Beast and human victim fell together. Two others were
dead and several bore bad wounds, but the remaining
warriors fought on, swords and armor smeared with
crimson. The narrow passage stank of ape, of sweat,
and of blood. Elric pressed into the fight, chopping at
the skull of an ape which grappled with Hown Serpent-
tamer, who had lost his sword. Hown darted a look of
thanks at Elric as he bent to retrieve his blade and together they set upon the largest of all the baboons. This
creature stood much taller than Elric and had Erekosë

pressed against the wall, Erekosë's sword through its shoulder.

From two sides, Hown and Elric stabbed and the baboon snarled and screamed, turning to face the new attackers, Erekosë's blade quivering in its shoulder. It rushed upon them and they stabbed again together, taking the monster in its heart and its lung so that when it roared at them blood vomited from its mouth. It fell to its knees, its eyes dimming, then sank slowly down.

And now there was silence in the passage and death lay all about them.

Terndrik of Hasghan was dead. Two of Corum's party were dead. All of Erekosë's surviving men bore major wounds. One of Hawkmoon's men was dead, but the remaining three were virtually unscathed. Brut of Lashmar's helm was dented, but he was otherwise unwounded and Ashnar the Lynx was disheveled, nothing more. Ashnar had taken two of the baboons during the fight. But now the barbarian's eyes rolled as he leaned, panting, against the wall.

"I begin to suspect this venture of being uneconomical," he said with a half-grin. He rallied himself, stepping over a baboon's corpse to join Elric. "The less time we take over it, the better. What think you, Elric?"

"I would agree." Elric returned his grin. "Come." And he led the way through the passage and into a chamber whose walls gave off a pinkish light. He had not walked far before he felt something catch at his ankle and he stared down in horror to see a long, thin snake winding itself about his leg. It was too late to use his sword; instead he seized the reptile behind its head and dragged it partially free of his leg before hacking the head from the body. The others were now stamping and shouting warnings to each other. The snakes did not appear to be venomous, but there were thousands of them, appearing, it seemed, from out of the floor itself. They were flesh-colored and had no eyes, more closely resembling earthworms than ordinary reptiles, but they were strong enough.

Hown Serpent-tamer sang a strange song now, with

many liquid, hissing notes, and this seemed to have a calming effect upon the creatures. One by one at first and then in increasing numbers, they dropped back to the floor, apparently sleeping. Hown grinned at his success.

Elric said, "Now I understand how you came by your surname."

"I was not sure the song would work on these," Hown told him, "for they are unlike any serpents I have ever seen in the seas of my own world."

They waded on through mounds of sleeping serpents, noticing that the next passage rose sharply. At times they were forced to use their hands to steady themselves as they climbed the peculiar, slippery material of the floor.

It was much hotter in this passage and they were all sweating, pausing several times to rest and mop their brows. The passage seemed to extend upward forever, turning occasionally, but never leveling out for more than a few feet. At times it narrowed to little more than a tube through which they had to squirm on their stomachs and at other times the roof disappeared into the gloom over their heads. Elric had long since given up trying to relate their position to what he had seen of the outside of the castle. From time to time small, shapeless creatures rushed toward them in shoals apparently with the intention of attacking them, but these were rarely more than an irritation and were soon all but ignored by the party as it continued its climb.

For a while they had not heard the strange voice which had greeted them upon their entering, but now it began to whisper again, its tones more urgent than before.

"Where? Where? Oh, the pain!"

They paused, trying to locate the source of the voice, but it seemed to come from everywhere at once.

Grim-faced, they continued, plagued by thousands of little creatures which bit at their exposed flesh like so many gnats, yet the creatures were not insects. Elric had seen nothing like them before. They were shapeless, primitive, and all but colorless. They battered at his face as he moved; they were like a wind. Half-blinded, choked, sweating, he felt his strength leaving him. The air was so thick now, so hot, so salty, it was as if he moved through liquid. The others were as badly affected as was he; some were staggering and two men fell, to be helped up again by comrades almost as exhausted. Elric was tempted to strip off his armor, but he knew this would leave more of his flesh to the mercy of the little flying creatures.

Still they climbed and now more of the serpentine things they had seen earlier began to writhe around their feet, hampering them further, for all that Hown sang his sleeping song until he was hoarse.

"We can survive this only a little longer," said Ashnar the Lynx, moving close to Elric. "We shall be in no condition to meet the sorcerer if we ever find him or his sister."

Elric nodded a gloomy head. "My thoughts, too, yet what else may we do, Ashnar?"

"Nothing," said Ashnar in a low voice. "Nothing."

"Where? Where? Where?" The word rustled all about them. Many of the party were becoming openly nervous.

V

They had reached the top of the passage. The querulous voice was much louder now, but it quavered more. They saw an archway and beyond the archway a lighted chamber.

"Agak's room, without doubt," said Ashnar, taking a better grip on his sword.

"Possibly," said Elric. He felt detached from his body. Perhaps it was the heat and the exhaustion, or his growing sense of disquiet, but something made him withdraw into himself and hesitate before entering the chamber.

The place was octagonal and each of its eight sloping sides was of a different color and each color changed constantly. Occasionally the walls became semitransparent, revealing a complete view of the ruined city (or collection of cities) far below, and also a view of the twin castle to this one, still connected by tubes and wires.

It was the large pool in the center of the chamber which attracted their attention mostly. It seemed deep and was full of evil-smelling, viscous stuff. It bubbled. Shapes formed in it. Grotesque and strange, beautiful and familiar, the shapes seemed always upon the brink of taking permanent form before falling back into the stuff of the pool. And the voice was still louder and there was no question now that it came from the pool.

"What? What? Who invades?"

. Elric forced himself closer to the pool and for a moment saw his own face staring out at him before it melted.

"Who invades? Ah! I am too weak!"

Elric spoke to the pool. "We are of those you would destroy," he said. "We are those on whom you would feed."

"Ah! Agak! Agak! I am sick! Where are you?"

Ashnar and Brut joined Elric. The faces of the warriors were filled with disgust.

"Agak," growled Ashnar the Lynx, his eyes narrowing. "At last some sign that the sorcerer is here!"

The others had all crowded in, to stand as far away from the pool as possible, but all stared, fascinated by the variety of the shapes forming and disintegrating in the viscous liquid.

"I weaken. . . . My energy needs to be replenished. . . . We must begin now, Agak. . . . It took us so long to reach this place. I thought I could rest. But there is disease here. It fills my body. Agak. Awaken, Agak. Awaken!"

"Some servant of Agak's, charged with the defense of the chamber?" suggested Hown Serpent-tamer in a small voice.

But Elric continued to stare into the pool as he began, he thought, to realize the truth.

"Will Agak wake?" Brut said. "Will he come?" He glanced nervously around him.

"Agak!" called Ashnar the Lynx. "Coward!"

"Agak!" cried many of the other warriors, brandishing their swords.

But Elric said nothing and he noted, too, that Hawk-moon and Corum and Erekosë all remained silent. He guessed that they must be filled with the same dawning understanding.

He looked at them. In Erekosë's eyes he saw an agony, a pity both for himself and his comrades.

"We are the Four Who Are One," said Erekosë. His voice shook.

Elric was seized by an alien impulse, an impulse which disgusted and terrified him. "No. . . ." He attempted to sheathe Stormbringer, but the sword refused to enter its scabbard.

"*Agak! Quickly!*" said the voice from the pool.

"If we do not do this thing," said Erekosë, "they will eat all our worlds. Nothing will remain."

Elric put his free hand to his head. He swayed upon the edge of that frightful pool. He moaned.

"We must do it, then." Corum's voice was an echo.

"I will not," said Elric. "I am myself."

"And I!" said Hawkmoon.

But Corum Jhaelen Irsei said, "It is the only way for us, for the single thing that we are. Do you not see that? We are the only creatures of our worlds who possess the means of slaying the sorcerers—in the only manner in which they can be slain!"

Elric looked at Corum, at Hawkmoon, at Erekosë, and again he saw something of himself in all of them.

"We are the Four Who Are One," said Erekosë. "Our united strength is greater than the sum. We must come together, brothers. We must conquer here before we can hope to conquer Agak."

"No. . . ." Elric moved away, but somehow he found himself standing at a corner of the bubbling, noxious pool from which the voice still murmured and com-plained, in which shapes still formed, reformed, and faded. And at each of the other three corners stood one of his companions. All had a set, fatalistic look to them.

The warriors who had accompanied the Four drew back

to the walls. Otto Blendker and Brut of Lashmar stood near the doorway, listening for anything which might come up the passage to the chamber. Ashnar the Lynx fingered the brand at his belt, a look of pure horror on his rugged features.

Elric felt his arm begin to rise, drawn upward by his sword, and he saw that each of his three companions were also lifting their swords. The swords reached out across the pool and their tips met above the exact center.

Elric yelled as something entered his being. Again he tried to break free, but the power was too strong. Other voices spoke in his head.

"*I understand. . . .*" This was Corum's distant murmur. "*It is the only way.*"

"*Oh, no, no. . . .*" And this was Hawkmoon, but the words came from Elric's lips.

"*Agak!*" cried the pool. The stuff became more agitated, more alarmed. "*Agak! Quickly! Wake!*"

Elric's body began to shake, but his hand kept a firm hold upon the sword. The atoms of his body flew apart and then united again into a single flowing entity which traveled up the blade of the sword toward the apex. And Elric was still Elric, shouting with the terror of it, sighing with the ecstasy of it.

Elric was still Elric when he drew away from the pool and looked upon himself for a single moment, seeing himself wholly joined with his three other selves.

A being hovered over the pool. On each side of its head was a face and each face belonged to one of the companions. Serene and terrible, the eyes did not blink. It had eight arms and the arms were still; it squatted over the pool on eight legs, and its armor and accouterments were of all colors blending and at the same time separate.

The being clutched a single great sword in all eight hands and both he and the sword glowed with a ghastly golden light.

Then Elric had rejoined this body and had become a

different thing—himself and three others and something else which was the sum of that union.

The Four Who Were One reversed its monstrous sword so that the point was directed downward at the frenetically boiling stuff in the pool below. The stuff feared the sword. It mewled.

"Agak, Agak. . . ."

The being of whom Elric was a part gathered its great strength and began to plunge the sword down.

Shapeless waves appeared on the surface of the pool. Its whole color changed from sickly yellow to an unhealthy green. *"Agak, I die. . . ."*

Inexorably the sword moved down. It touched the surface.

The pool swept back and forth; it tried to ooze over the sides and onto the floor. The sword bit deeper and the Four Who Were One felt new strength flow up the blade. There came a moan; slowly the pool quieted. It became silent. It became still. It became gray.

Then the Four Who Were One descended into the pool to be absorbed.

It could see clearly now. It tested its body. It controlled every limb, every function. It had triumphed; it had revitalized the pool. Through its single octagonal eye it looked in all directions at the same time over the wide ruins of the city; then it focused all its attention upon its twin.

Agak had awakened too late, but he was awakening at last, roused by the dying cries of his sister Gagak, whose body the mortals had first invaded and whose intelligence they had overwhelmed, whose eye they now used and whose powers they would soon attempt to utilize.

Agak did not need to turn his head to look upon the being he still saw as his sister. Like hers, his intelligence was contained within the huge eight-sided eye.

"Did you call me, sister?"

"I spoke your name, that is all, brother." There were

enough vestiges of Gagak's life-force in the Four Who Were One for it to imitate her manner of speaking.

"You cried out?"

"A dream." The Four paused and then it spoke again: *"A disease. I dreamed that there was something upon this island which made me unwell."*

"Is that possible? We do not know sufficient about these dimensions or the creatures inhabiting them. Yet none is as powerful as Agak and Gagak. Fear not, sister. We must begin our work soon."

"It is nothing. Now I am awake."

Agak was puzzled. *"You speak oddly."*

"The dream . . ." answered the creature which had entered Gagak's body and destroyed her.

"We must begin," said Agak. *"The dimensions turn and the time has come. Ah, feel it. It waits for us to take it. So much rich energy. How we shall conquer when we go home!"*

"I feel it," replied the Four, and it did. It felt its whole universe, dimension upon dimension, swirling all about it. Stars and planets and moons through plane upon plane, all full of the energy upon which Agak and Gagak had desired to feed. And there was enough of Gagak still within the Four to make the Four experience a deep, anticipatory hunger which, now that the dimensions attained the right conjunction, would soon be satisfied.

The Four was tempted to join with Agak and feast, though it knew if it did so it would rob its own universe of every shred of energy. Stars would fade, worlds would die. Even the Lords of Law and Chaos would perish, for they were part of the same universe. Yet to possess such power it might be worth committing such a tremendous crime. . . . It controlled this desire and gathered itself for its attack before Agak became too wary.

"Shall we feast, sister?"

The Four realized that the ship had brought it to the island at exactly the proper moment. Indeed, they had almost come too late.

"Sister?" Agak was again puzzled. *"What . . . ?"*

The Four knew it must disconnect from Agak. The

tubes and wires fell away from his body and were with-
drawn into Gagak's.

"What's this?" Agak's strange body trembled for a
moment. *"Sister?"*

The Four prepared itself. For all that it had absorbed
Gagak's memories and instincts, it was still not confident
that it would be able to attack Agak in her chosen form.
And since the sorceress had possessed the power to
change her form, the Four began to change, groaning
greatly, experiencing dreadful pain, drawing all the materials of its stolen being together so that what had appeared to be a building now became pulpy, unformed
flesh. And Agak, stunned, looked on.

"Sister? Your sanity . . ."

The building, the creature that was Gagak, threshed,
melted, and erupted. It screamed in agony.

It attained its form.

It laughed.

Four faces laughed upon a gigantic head. Eight arms
waved in triumph, eight legs began to move. And over
that head it waved a single, massive sword.

And it was running.

It ran upon Agak while the alien sorcerer was still in
his static form. Its sword was whirling and shards of
ghastly golden light fell away from it as it moved, lashing the shadowed landscape. The Four was as large as
Agak. And at this moment it was as strong.

But Agak, realizing his danger, began to suck. No
longer would this be a pleasurable ritual shared with his
sister. He must suck at the energy of this universe if he
were to find the strength to defend himself, to gain what
he needed to destroy his attacker, the slayer of his sister.
Worlds died as Agak sucked.

But not enough. Agak tried cunning.

*"This is the center of your universe. All its dimen-
sions intersect here. Come, you can share the power. My
sister is dead. I accept her death. You shall be my partner
now. With this power we shall conquer a universe far
richer than this!"*

"No!" said the Four, still advancing.

"Very well, but be assured of your defeat."

The Four swung its sword. The sword fell upon the faceted eye within which Agak's intelligence-pool bubbled, just as his sister's had once bubbled. But Agak was stronger already and healed himself at once.

Agak's tendrils emerged and lashed at the Four and the Four cut at the tendrils as it sought his body. And Agak sucked more energy to himself. His body, which the mortals had mistaken for a building, began to glow burning scarlet and to radiate an impossible heat.

The sword roared and flared so that black light mingled with the gold and flowed against the scarlet. And all the while the Four could sense its own universe shrinking and dying.

"Give back, Agak, what you have stolen!" said the Four.

Planes and angles and curves, wires and tubes, flickered with deep red heat and Agak sighed. The universe whimpered.

"I am stronger than you," said Agak. *"Now."*

And Agak sucked again.

The Four knew that Agak's attention was diverted for just that short while as he fed. And the Four knew that it, too, must draw energy from its own universe if Agak were to be defeated. So the sword was raised.

The sword was flung back, its blade slicing through tens of thousands of dimensions and drawing their power to it. Then it began to swing back. It swung and black light bellowed from its blade. It swung and Agak became aware of it. His body began to alter. Down toward the sorcerer's great eye, down toward Agak's intelligence-pool swept the black blade.

Agak's many tendrils rose to defend the sorcerer against the sword, but the sword cut through them as if they were not there and it struck the eight-sided chamber which was Agak's eyes and it plunged on down into Agak's intelligence-pool, deep into the stuff of the sorcerer's sensibility, drawing up Agak's energy into itself and thence into its master, the Four Who Were One. And something screamed through the universe and something sent a tremor through the universe. And the universe was dead, even as Agak began to die.

The Four did not dare wait to see if Agak were completely vanquished. It swept the sword out, back through the dimensions, and everywhere the blade touched the energy was restored. The sword rang round and round, round and round, dispersing the energy. And the sword sang its triumph and its glee.

And little shreds of black and golden light whispered away and were reabsorbed.

For a moment the universe had been dead. Now it lived and Agak's energy had been added to it.

Agak lived, too, but he was frozen. He had attempted to change his shape. Now he still half-resembled the building Elric had seen when he first came to the island, but part of him resembled the Four Who Were One—here was part of Corum's face, here a leg, there a fragment of sword-blade—as if Agak had believed, at the end, that the Four could only be defeated if its own form were assumed, just as the Four had assumed Gagak's form.

"We had waited so long. . . ." Agak sighed and then he was dead.

And the Four sheathed its sword.

Then there came a howling through the ruins of the many cities and a strong wind blustered against the body of the Four so that it was forced to kneel on its eight legs and bow its four-faced head before the gale. Then, gradually, it reassumed the shape of Gagak, the sorceress, and then it lay within Gagak's stagnating intelligence-pool and then it rose over it, hovered for a moment, withdrew its sword from the pool. Then four beings fled apart and Elric and Hawkmoon and Erekosë and Corum stood with sword-blades touching over the center of the dead brain.

The four men sheathed their swords. They stared for a second into each other's eyes and all saw terror and awe there. Elric turned away.

He could find neither thoughts nor emotions in him which would relate to what had happened. There were

no words he could use. He stood looking dumbly at Ashnar the Lynx and he wondered why Ashnar giggled and
chewed at his beard and scraped at the flesh of his own
face with his fingernails, his sword forgotten upon the
floor of the gray chamber.

"Now I have flesh again. Now I have flesh," Ashnar
kept saying.

Elric wondered why Hown Serpent-tamer lay curled in
a ball at Ashnar's feet, and why when Brut of Lashmar
emerged from the passage he fell down and lay stretched
upon the floor, stirring a little and moaning as if in
disturbed slumber. Otto Blendker came into the chamber.
His sword was in its scabbard. His eyes were tight shut
and he hugged at himself, shivering.

Elric thought to himself: *I must forget all this or
sanity will disappear forever.*

He went to Brut and helped the blond warrior to his
feet. "What did you see?"

"More than I deserved, for all my sins. We were
trapped—trapped in that skull. . . ." Then Brut began
to weep as a small child might weep and Elric took the
tall warrior in his own arms and stroked his head and
could not find words or sounds with which to comfort
him.

"We must go," said Erekosë. His eyes were glazed. He
staggered as he walked.

Thus, dragging those who had fainted, leading those
who had gone mad, leaving those who had died behind,
they fled through the dead passages of Gagak's body, no
longer plagued by the things she had created in her attempt to rid that body of those she had experienced as
an invading disease. The passages and chambers were
cold and brittle and the men were glad when they stood
outside and saw the ruins, the sourceless shadows, the
red, static sun.

Otto Blendker was the only one of the warriors who
seemed to retain his sanity through the ordeal, when
they had been absorbed, unknowingly, into the body of
the Four Who Were One. He dragged his brand from his
belt and he took out his tinder and ignited it. Soon the

brand was flaming and the others lighted theirs from his. Elric trudged to where Agak's remains still lay and he shuddered as he recognized in a monstrous stone face part of his own features. He felt that the stuff could not possibly burn, but it did. Behind him Gagak's body blazed, too. They were swiftly consumed and pillars of growling fire jutted into the sky, sending up a smoke of white and crimson which for a little while obscured the red disk of the sun.

The men watched the corpses burn.

"I wonder," said Corum, "if the captain knew why he sent us here?"

"Or if he suspected what would happen?" said Hawkmoon. Hawkmoon's tone was near to resentful.

"Only we—only that being—could battle Agak and Gagak in anything resembling their own terms," said Erekosë. "Other means would not have been successful, no other creature could have the particular qualities, the enormous power needed to slay such strange sorcerers."

"So it seems," said Elric, and he would talk no more of it.

"Hopefully," said Corum, "you will forget this experience as you forgot—or will forget—the other."

Elric offered him a hard stare. "Hopefully, brother," he said.

Erekosë's chuckle was ironic. "Who could recall that?" And he, too, said no more.

Ashnar the Lynx, who had ceased his gigglings as he watched the fire, shrieked suddenly and broke away from the main party. He ran toward the flickering column and then veered away, disappearing among the ruins and the shadows.

Otto Blendker gave Elric a questioning stare, but Elric shook his head. "Why follow him? What can we do for him?" He looked down at Hown Serpent-tamer. He had particularly liked the man in the sea-green armor. He shrugged.

When they moved on, they left the curled body of

Hown Serpent-tamer where it lay, helping only Brut of
Lashmar across the rubble and down to the shore.

Soon they saw the white mist ahead and knew they
neared the sea, though the ship was not in sight.

At the edge of the mist both Hawkmoon and Erekosë
paused.

"I will not rejoin the ship," said Hawkmoon. "I feel
I've served my passage now. If I can find Tanelorn, this,
I suspect, is where I must look."

"My own feelings." Erekosë nodded his head.

Elric looked to Corum. Corum smiled. "I have already
found Tanelorn. I go back to the ship in the hope
that soon it will deposit me upon a more familiar shore."

"That is my hope," said Elric. His arm still supported
Brut of Lashmar.

Brut whispered, "What was it? What happened to us?"

Elric increased his grip upon the warrior's shoulder.
"Nothing," he said.

Then, as Elric tried to lead Brut into the mist, the
blond warrior stepped back, breaking free. "I will
stay," he said. He moved away from Elric. "I am
sorry."

Elric was puzzled. "Brut?"

"I am sorry," Brut said again. "I fear you. I fear that
ship."

Elric made to follow the warrior, but Corum put a
hard silver hand upon his shoulder. "Comrade, let us be
gone from this place." His smile was bleak. "It is what
is back there that I fear more than the ship."

They stared over the ruins. In the distance they could
see the remains of the fire and there were two shadows
there now, the shadows of Gagak and Agak as they
had first appeared to them.

Elric drew a cold breath of air. "With that I agree," he
told Corum.

Otto Blendker was the only warrior who chose to return to the ship with them. "If that is Tanelorn, it
is not, after all, the place I sought," he said.

Soon they were waist-deep in the water. They saw

again the outlines of the dark ship; they saw the captain leaning on the rail, his arm raised as if in salute to someone or something upon the island.

"Captain," called Corum, "we come aboard."

"You are welcome," said the captain. "Yes, you are welcome." The blind face turned toward them as Elric reached out for the rope ladder. "Would you care to sail for a while into the silent places, the restful places?"

"I think so," said Elric. He paused, halfway up the ladder, and he touched his head. "I have many wounds."

He reached the rail and with his own cool hands the captain helped him over. "They will heal, Elric."

Elric moved closer to the mast. He leaned against it and watched the silent crew as they unfurled the sail. Corum and Otto Blendker came aboard. Elric listened to the sharp sound of the anchor as it was drawn up. The ship swayed a little.

Otto Blendker looked at Elric, then at the captain, then he turned and went into his cabin, saying nothing at all as he closed the door.

The sail filled, the ship began to move. The captain reached out and found Elric's arm. He took Corum's arm, too, and led them toward his cabin. "The wine," he said. "It will heal all the wounds."

At the door of the captain's cabin Elric paused. "And does the wine have other properties?" he asked. "Does it cloud a man's reason? Was it that which made me accept your commission, Captain?"

The captain shrugged. "What is reason?"

The ship was gathering speed. The white mist was thicker and a cold wind blew at the rags of cloth and metal Elric wore. He sniffed, thinking for a moment that he smelled smoke upon that wind.

He put his two hands to his face and touched his flesh. His face was cold. He let his hands fall to his sides and he followed the captain into the warmth of the cabin.

The captain poured wine into silver cups from his silver jug. He stretched out a hand to offer a cup to Elric and to Corum. They drank.

A little later the captain said, "How do you feel?"

Elric said, "I feel nothing."

And that night he dreamed only of shadows and in the morning he could not understand his dream at all.

Book TWO

SAILING TO
THE PRESENT

I

His bone-white, long-fingered hand upon a carved demon's head in black-brown hardwood (one of the few such decorations to be found anywhere about the vessel), the tall man stood alone in the ship's fo'c'sle and stared through large, slanting crimson eyes at the mist into which they moved with a speed and sureness to make any mortal mariner marvel and become incredulous.

There were sounds in the distance, incongruent with the sounds of even this nameless, timeless sea: thin sounds, agonized and terrible, for all that they remained remote—yet the ship followed them, as if drawn by them; they grew louder—pain and despair were there, but terror was predominant.

Elric had heard such sounds echoing from his cousin Yyrkoon's sardonically named "Pleasure Chambers" in the days before he had fled the responsibilities of ruling all that remained of the old Melnibonéan Empire. These were the voices of men whose very souls were under siege; men to whom death meant not mere extinction, but a continuation of existence, forever in thrall to some cruel and supernatural master. He had heard men cry so when his salvation and his nemesis, his great black battle-blade Stormbringer, drank their souls.

He did not savor the sound: he hated it, turned his back away from the source and was about to descend the ladder to the main deck when he realized that Otto Blendker had come up behind him. Now that Corum had been borne off by friends with chariots which could ride upon the surface of the water, Blendker was the last of those comrades to have fought at Elric's side against the two alien sorcerers Gagak and Agak.

Blendker's black, scarred face was troubled. The ex-

scholar, turned hireling sword, covered his ears with his
huge palms.

"Ach! By the Twelve Symbols of Reason, Elric, who
makes that din? It's as though we sail close to the shores
of Hell itself!"

Prince Elric of Melniboné shrugged. "I'd be prepared
to forego an answer and leave my curiosity unsatisfied,
Master Blendker, if only our ship would change course.
As it is, we sail closer and closer to the source."

Blendker grunted his agreement. "I've no wish to encounter whatever it is that causes those poor fellows to
scream so! Perhaps we should inform the captain."

"You think he does not know where his own ship sails?"
Elric's smile had little humor.

The tall black man rubbed at the inverted V-shaped
scar which ran from his forehead to his jawbones. "I
wonder if he plans to put us into battle again."

"I'll not fight another for him." Elric's hand moved
from the carved rail to the pommel of his runesword. "I
have business of my own to attend to, once I'm back on
real land."

A wind came from nowhere. There was a sudden rent
in the mist. Now Elric could see that the ship sailed
through rust-colored water. Peculiar lights gleamed in
that water, just below the surface. There was an impression of creatures moving ponderously in the depths of
the ocean and, for a moment, Elric thought he glimpsed
a white, bloated face not dissimilar to his own—a Melnibonéan face. Impulsively he whirled, back to the rail,
looking past Blendker as he strove to control the nausea
in his throat.

For the first time since he had come aboard the
Dark Ship he was able clearly to see the length of the
vessel. Here were the two great wheels, one beside him
on the foredeck, one at the far end of the ship on the
reardeck, tended now as always by the steersman, the
captain's sighted twin. There was the great mast bearing
the taut black sail, and fore and aft of this, the two deck
cabins, one of which was entirely empty (its occupants
having been killed during their last landfall) and one of

which was occupied only by himself and Blendker. Elric's gaze was drawn back to the steersman and not for
the first time the albino wondered how much influence
the captain's twin had over the course of the Dark Ship.
The man seemed tireless, rarely, to Elric's knowledge,
going below to his quarters, which occupied the stern
deck as the captain's occupied the foredeck. Once or
twice Elric or Blendker had tried to involve the steersman in conversation, but he appeared to be as dumb
as his brother was blind.

The cryptographic, geometrical carvings covering all
the ship's wood and most of its metal, from sternpost
to figurehead, were picked out by the shreds of pale
mist still clinging to them (and again Elric wondered if
the ship actually generated the mist normally surrounding it) and, as he watched, the designs slowly turned to
pale pink fire as the light from that red star, which forever followed them, permeated the overhead cloud.

A noise from below. The captain, his long red-gold
hair drifting in a breeze which Elric could not feel,
emerged from his cabin. The captain's circlet of blue jade,
worn like a diadem, had turned to something of a violet
shade in the pink light, and even his buff-colored hose
and tunic reflected the hue—even the silver sandals with
their silver lacing glittered with the rosy tint.

Again Elric looked upon that mysterious blind face, as
unhuman, in the accepted sense, as his own, and puzzled
upon the origin of the one who would allow himself to
be called nothing but "Captain."

As if at the captain's summons, the mist drew itself
about the ship again, as a woman might draw a froth of
furs about her body. The red star's light faded, but the
distant screams continued.

Did the captain notice the screams now for the first
time, or was this a pantomime of surprise? His blind
head tilted, a hand went to his ear. He murmured in a
tone of satisfaction, "Aha!" The head lifted. "Elric?"

"Here," said the albino. "Above you."

"We are almost there, Elric."

The apparently fragile hand found the rail of the companionway. The captain began to climb.

Elric faced him at the top of the ladder. "If it's a battle . . ."

The captain's smile was enigmatic, bitter. "It was a fight—or shall be one."

". . . we'll have no part of it," concluded the albino firmly.

"It is not one of the battles in which my ship is directly involved," the blind man reassured him. "Those whom you can hear are the vanquished—lost in some future which, I think, you will experience close to the end of your present incarnation."

Elric waved a dismissive hand. "I'll be glad, Captain, if you would cease such vapid mystification. I'm weary of it."

"I'm sorry it offends you. I answer literally, according to my instincts."

The captain, going past Elric and Otto Blendker so that he could stand at the rail, seemed to be apologizing. He said nothing for a while, but listened to the disturbing and confused babble from the mist. Then he nodded, apparently satisfied.

"We'll sight land shortly. If you would disembark and seek your own world, I should advise you to do so now. This is the closest we shall ever come again to your plane."

Elric let his anger show. He cursed, invoking Arioch's name, and put a hand upon the blind man's shoulder. "What? You cannot return me directly to my own plane?"

"It is too late." The captain's dismay was apparently genuine. "The ship sails on. We near the end of our long voyage."

"But how shall I find my world? I have no sorcery great enough to move me between the spheres! And demonic assistance is denied me here."

"There is one gateway to your world," the captain told him. "That is why I suggest you disembark. Elsewhere there are none at all. Your sphere and this one intersect directly."

"But you say this lies in my future."

"Be sure—you will return to your own time. Here you are timeless. It is why your memory is so poor. It is why you remember so little of what befalls you. Seek for the gateway—it is crimson and it emerges from the sea off the coast of the island."

"Which island?"

"The one we approach."

Elric hesitated. "And where shall you go, when I have landed?"

"To Tanelorn," said the captain. "There is something I must do there. My brother and I must complete our destiny. We carry cargo as well as men. Many will try to stop us now, for they fear our cargo. We might perish, but yet we must do all we can to reach Tanelorn."

"Was that not, then, Tanelorn, where we fought Agak and Gagak?"

"That was nothing more than a broken dream of Tanelorn, Elric."

The Melnibonéan knew that he would receive no more information from the captain.

"You offer me a poor choice—to sail with you into danger and never see my own world again, or to risk landing on yonder island inhabited, by the sound of it, by the damned and those which prey upon the damned!"

The captain's blind eyes moved in Elric's direction. "I know," he said softly. "But it is the best I can offer you, nonetheless."

The screams, the imploring, terrified shouts, were closer now, but there were fewer of them. Glancing over the side, Elric thought he saw a pair of armored hands rising from the water; there was foam, red-flecked and noxious, and there was yellowish scum in which pieces of frightful flotsam drifted; there were broken timbers, scraps of canvas, tatters of flags and clothing, fragments of weapons, and, increasingly, there were floating corpses.

"But where was the battle?" Blendker whispered, fascinated and horrified by the sight.

"Not on this plane," the captain told him. "You see only the wreckage which has drifted over from one world to another."

"Then it was a supernatural battle?"

The captain smiled again. "I am not omniscient. But, yes, I believe there were supernatural agencies involved. The warriors of half a world fought in the sea-battle—to decide the fate of the multiverse. It is—or will be—one of the decisive battles to determine the fate of Mankind, to fix Man's destiny for the coming Cycle."

"Who were the participants?" asked Elric, voicing the question in spite of his resolve. "What were the issues as they understood them?"

"You will know in time, I think." The captain's head faced the sea again.

Blendker sniffed the air. "Ach! It's foul!"

Elric, too, found the odor increasingly unpleasant. Here and there now the water was lighted by guttering fires which revealed the faces of the drowning, some of whom still managed to cling to pieces of blackened driftwood. Not all the faces were human (though they had the appearance of having, once, been human): Things with the snouts of pigs and of bulls raised twisted hands to the Dark Ship and grunted plaintively for succor, but the captain ignored them and the steersman held his course.

Fires spluttered and water hissed; smoke mingled with the mist. Elric had his sleeve over his mouth and nose and was glad that the smoke and mist between them helped obscure the sights, for as the wreckage grew thicker not a few of the corpses he saw reminded him more of reptiles than of men, their pale, lizard bellies spilling something other than blood.

"If that is my future," Elric told the captain, "I've a mind to remain on board, after all."

"You have a duty, as have I," said the captain quietly. "The future must be served, as much as the past and the present."

Elric shook his head. "I fled the duties of an empire because I sought freedom," the albino told him. "And freedom I must have."

"No," murmured the captain. "There is no such thing. Not yet. Not for us. We must go through much more before we can even begin to guess what freedom is. The price for the knowledge alone is probably higher than any you would care to pay at this stage of your life. Indeed, life itself is often the price."

"I also sought release from metaphysics when I left Melniboné," said Elric. "I'll get the rest of my gear and take the land that's offered. With luck this Crimson Gate will be quickly found and I'll be back among dangers and torments which will, at least, be familiar."

"It is the only decision you could have made." The captain's blind head turned toward Blendker. "And you, Otto Blendker? What shall you do?"

"Elric's world is not mine and I like not the sound of those screams. What can you promise me, sir, if I sail on with you?"

"Nothing but a good death." There was regret in the captain's voice.

"Death is the promise we're all born with, sir. A good death is better than a poor one. I'll sail on with you."

"As you like. I think you're wise." The captain sighed. "I'll say farewell to you, then, Elric of Melniboné. You fought well in my service and I thank you."

"Fought for what?" Elric asked.

"Oh, call it Mankind. Call it Fate. Call it a dream or an ideal, if you wish."

"Shall I never have a clearer answer?"

"Not from me. I do not think there is one."

"You allow a man little faith." Elric began to descend the companionway.

"There are two kinds of faith, Elric. Like freedom, there is a kind which is easily kept but proves not worth the keeping, and there is a kind which is hard-won. I agree, I offer little of the former."

Elric strode toward his cabin. He laughed, feeling genuine affection for the blind man at that moment. "I

thought I had a penchant for such ambiguities, but I
have met my match in you, Captain."

He noticed that the steersman had left his place at
the wheel and was swinging out a boat on its davits, pre-
paratory to lowering it.

"Is that for me?"

The steersman nodded.

Elric ducked into his cabin. He was leaving the ship
with nothing but that which he had brought aboard, only
his clothing and his armor were in a poorer state of re-
pair than they had been, and his mind was in a considerably greater state of confusion.

Without hesitation he gathered up his things, drawing
his heavy cloak about him, pulling on his gauntlets,
fastening buckles and thongs, then he left the cabin and
returned to the deck. The captain was pointing through
the mist at the dark outlines of a coast. "Can you see
land, Elric?"

"I can."

"You must go quickly, then."

"Willingly."

Elric swung himself over the rail and into the boat.
The boat struck the side of the ship several times, so
that the hull boomed like the beating of some huge
funeral drum. Otherwise there was silence now upon the
misty waters and no sign of wreckage.

Blendker saluted him. "I wish you luck, comrade."

"You, too, Master Blendker."

The boat began to sink toward the flat surface of the
sea, the pulleys of the davits creaking. Elric clung to the
rope, letting go as the boat hit the water. He stumbled
and sat down heavily upon the seat, releasing the
ropes so that the boat drifted at once away from the Dark
Ship. He got out the oars and fitted them into their row-
locks.

As he pulled toward the shore he heard the captain's
voice calling to him, but the words were muffled by the
mist and he would never know, now, if the blind man's
last communication had been a warning or merely
some formal pleasantry. He did not care. The boat moved

smoothly through the water; the mist began to thin, but so, too, did the light fade.

Suddenly he was under a twilight sky, the sun already gone and stars appearing. Before he had reached the shore it was already completely dark, with the moon not yet risen, and it was with difficulty that he beached the boat on what seemed flat rocks, and stumbled inland until he judged himself safe enough from any inrushing tide.

Then, with a sigh, he lay down, thinking just to order his thoughts before moving on; but, almost instantly, he was asleep.

Elric dreamed.

He dreamed not merely of the end of his world but of the end of an entire cycle in the history of the cosmos. He dreamed that he was not only Elric of Melniboné but that he was other men, too—men who were pledged to some numinous cause which even they could not describe. And he dreamed that he had dreamed of the Dark Ship and Tanelorn and Agak and Gagak while he lay exhausted upon a beach somewhere beyond the borders of Pikarayd; and when he woke up he was smiling sardonically, congratulating himself for the possession of a grandiose imagination. But he could not clear his head entirely of the impression left by that dream.

This shore was not the same, so plainly something had befallen him—perhaps he had been drugged by slavers, then later abandoned when they found him not what they expected. . . . But, no, the explanation would not do. If he could discover his whereabouts, he might also recall the true facts.

It was dawn, for certain. He sat up and looked about him.

He was sprawled upon a dark, sea-washed limestone

pavement, cracked in a hundred places, the cracks so deep that the small streams of foaming salt water rushing through these many narrow channels made raucous what would otherwise have been a very still morning.

Elric climbed to his feet, using his scabbarded runesword to steady himself. His bone-white lids closed for a moment over his crimson eyes as he sought, again, to recollect the events which had brought him here.

He recalled his flight from Pikarayd, his panic, his falling into a coma of hopelessness, his dreams. And, because he was evidently neither dead nor a prisoner, he could at least conclude that his pursuers had, after all, given up the chase, for if they had found him they would have killed him.

Opening his eyes and casting about him, he remarked the peculiar blue quality of the light (doubtless a trick of the sun behind the gray clouds) which made the landscape ghastly and gave the sea a dull, metallic look.

The limestone terraces which rose from the sea and stretched above him shone intermittently, like polished lead. On an impulse he held his hand to the light and inspected it. The normally lusterless white of his skin was now tinged with a faint, bluish luminosity. He found it pleasing and smiled as a child might smile, in innocent wonder.

He had expected to be tired, but he now realized that he felt unusually refreshed, as if he had slept long after a good meal, and, deciding not to question the fact of this fortunate (and unlikely) gift, he determined to climb the cliffs in the hope that he might get some idea of his bearings before he decided which direction he would take.

Limestone could be a little treacherous, but it made easy climbing, for there was almost always somewhere that one terrace met another.

He climbed carefully and steadily, finding many footholds, and seemed to gain considerable height quite quickly, yet it was noon before he had reached the top and found himself standing at the edge of a broad, rocky plateau which fell away sharply to form a close horizon. Beyond the plateau was only the sky. Save for sparse, brownish grass, little grew here and there were no signs at all of human habitation. It was now, for the first time, that Elric realized the absence of any form of wildlife. Not a single seabird flew in the air, not an insect crept through the grass. Instead, there was an enormous silence hanging over the brown plain.

Elric was still remarkably untired, so he decided to make the best use he could of his energy and reach the edge of the plateau in the hope that, from there, he would sight a town or a village. He pressed on, feeling no lack of food and water, and his stride was singularly energetic, still; but he had misjudged his distance and the sun had begun to set well before his journey to the edge was completed. The sky on all sides turned a deep, velvety blue and the few clouds that there were in it were also tinged blue, and now, for the first time, Elric realized that the sun itself was not its normal shade, that it burned blackish purple, and he wondered again if he still dreamed.

The ground began to rise sharply and it was with some effort that he walked, but before the light had completely faded he was on the steep flank of a hill, descending toward a wide valley which, though bereft of trees, contained a river which wound through rocks and russet turf and bracken.

After a short rest, Elric decided to press on, although night had fallen, and see if he could reach the river where he might at least drink and, possibly, in the morning find fish to eat.

Again, no moon appeared to aid his progress and he walked for two or three hours in a darkness which was almost total, stumbling occasionally into large rocks, until the ground leveled and he felt sure he had reached the floor of the valley.

He had developed a strong thirst by now and was feeling somewhat hungry, but decided that it might be best to wait until morning before seeking the river when, rounding a particularly tall rock, he saw, with some astonishment, the light of a camp fire.

Hopefully this would be the fire of a company of merchants, a trading caravan on its way to some civilized country which would allow him to travel with it, perhaps in return for his services as a mercenary swordsman (it would not be the first time, since he had left Melniboné, that he had earned his bread in such a way).

Yet Elric's old instincts did not desert him; he approached the fire cautiously and let no one see him. Beneath an overhang of rock, made shadowy by the flame's light, he stood and observed the group of fifteen or sixteen men who sat or lay close to the fire, playing some kind of game involving dice and slivers of numbered ivory.

Gold, bronze, and silver gleamed in the firelight as the men staked large sums on the fall of a dice and the turn of a slip of ivory.

Elric guessed that, if they had not been so intent on their game, these men must certainly have detected his approach, for they were not, after all, merchants. By the evidence, they were warriors, wearing scarred leather and dented metal, their weapons ready to hand, yet they belonged to no army—unless it be an army of bandits—for they were of all races and (oddly) seemed to be from various periods in the history of the Young Kingdoms.

It was as if they had looted some scholar's collection of relics. An axman of the later Lormyrian Republic, which had come to an end some two hundred years ago, lay with his shoulder rubbing the elbow of a Chalalite bowman, from a period roughly contemporary with Elric's own. Close to the Chalalite sat a short Ilmioran infantryman of a century past. Next to him was a Filkharian in the barbaric dress of that nation's earliest times. Tarkeshites, Shazarians, Vilmirians, all mingled and the only thing they had in common, by the look of them, was a villainous, hungry cast to their features.

In other circumstances Elric might have skirted this encampment and moved on, but he was so glad to find human beings of any sort that he ignored the disturbing incongruities of the group; yet he remained content to watch them.

One of the men, less unwholesome than the others, was a bulky, black-bearded, baldheaded sea-warrior clad in the casual leathers and silks of the people of the Purple Towns. It was when this man produced a large gold Melnibonéan wheel—a coin not minted, as most coins, but carved by craftsmen to a design both ancient and intricate—that Elric's caution was fully conquered by his curiosity.

Very few of those coins existed in Melniboné and none, that Elric had heard of, outside; for the coins were not used for trade with the Young Kingdoms. They were prized, even by the nobility of Melniboné.

It seemed to Elric that the baldheaded man could only have acquired the coin from another Melnibonéan traveler—and Elric knew of no other Melnibonéans who shared his penchant for exploration. His wariness dismissed, he stepped into the circle.

If he had not been completely obsessed by the thought of the Melnibonéan wheel he might have taken some satisfaction in the sudden scuffle to arms which resulted. Within seconds, the majority of the men were on their feet, their weapons drawn.

For a moment, the gold wheel was forgotten. His hand upon his runesword's pommel, he presented the other in a placatory gesture.

"Forgive the interruption, gentlemen. I am but one tired fellow soldier who seeks to join you. I would beg some information and purchase some food, if you have it to spare."

On foot, the warriors had an even more ruffianly appearance. They grinned among themselves, entertained by Elric's courtesy but not impressed by it.

One, in the feathered helmet of a Pan Tangian sea-chief, with features to match—swarthy, sinister—pushed his head forward on its long neck and said banteringly:

"We've company enough, white-face. And few here are overfond of the man-demons of Melniboné. You must be rich."

Elric recalled the animosity with which Melnibonéans were regarded in the Young Kingdoms, particularly by those from Pan Tang who envied the Dragon Isle her power and her wisdom and, of late, had begun crudely to imitate Melniboné.

Increasingly on his guard, he said evenly, "I have a little money."

"Then we'll take it, demon." The Pan Tangian presented a dirty palm just below Elric's nose as he growled, "Give it over and be on your way."

Elric's smile was polite and fastidious, as if he had been told a poor joke.

The Pan Tangian evidently thought the joke better than did Elric, for he laughed heartily and looked to his nearest fellows for approval.

Coarse laughter infected the night and only the bald-headed, black-bearded man did not join in the jest, but took a step or two backward, while all the others pressed forward.

The Pan Tangian's face was close to Elric's own; his breath was foul and Elric saw that his beard and hair were alive with lice, yet he kept his head, replying in the same equable tone:

"Give me some decent food, a flask of water—some wine, if you have it—and I'll gladly give you the money I have."

The laughter rose and fell again as Elric continued:

"But if you would take my money and leave me with naught—then I must defend myself. I have a good sword."

The Pan Tangian strove to imitate Elric's irony. "But you will note, Sir Demon, that we outnumber you. Considerably."

Softly the albino spoke: "I've noticed that fact, but I'm not disturbed by it," and he had drawn the black blade even as he finished speaking, for they had come at him with a rush.

And the Pan Tangian was the first to die, sliced through the side, his vertebrae sheared, and Stormbringer, having taken its first soul, began to sing.

A Chalalite died next, leaping with stabbing javelin poised, on the point of the runesword, and Stormbringer murmured with pleasure.

But it was not until it had sliced the head clean off a Filkharian pike-master that the sword began to croon and come fully to life, black fire flickering up and down its length, its strange runes glowing.

Now the warriors knew they battled sorcery and became more cautious, yet they scarcely paused in their attack, and Elric, thrusting and parrying, hacking and slicing, needed all of the fresh, dark energy the sword passed on to him.

Lance, sword, ax, and dirk were blocked, wounds were given and received, but the dead had not yet outnumbered the living when Elric found himself with his back against the rock and nigh a dozen sharp weapons seeking his vitals.

It was at this point, when Elric had become somewhat less than confident that he could best so many, that the baldheaded warrior, ax in one gloved hand, sword in the other, came swiftly into the firelight and set upon those of his fellows closest to him.

"I thank you, sir!" Elric was able to shout, during the short respite this sudden turn produced. His morale improved, he resumed the attack.

The Lormyrian was cleaved from hip to pelvis as he dodged a feint; a Filkharian, who should have been dead four hundred years before, fell with the blood bubbling from lips and nostrils, and the corpses began to pile one upon the other. Still Stormbringer sang its sinister battle-song and still the runesword passed its power to its master so that with every death Elric found strength to slay more of the soldiers.

Those who remained now began to express their regret for their hasty attack. Where oaths and threats had issued from their mouths, now came plaintive petitions for mercy and those who had laughed with such bold braggadocio now wept like young girls, but Elric, full of his old battle-joy, spared none.

Meanwhile the man from the Purple Towns, unaided by

sorcery, put ax and sword to good work and dealt with three more of his one-time comrades, exulting in his work as if he had nursed a taste for it for some time.

"Yoi! But this is worthwhile slaughter!" cried the black-bearded one.

And then that busy butchery was suddenly done and Elric realized that none were left save himself and his new ally, who stood leaning on his ax, panting and grinning like a hound at the kill, replacing a steel skullcap upon his pate from where it had fallen during the fight, and wiping a bloody sleeve over the sweat glistening on his brow, and saying, in a deep, good-humored tone:

"Well, now, it is we who are wealthy, of a sudden."

Elric sheathed a Stormbringer still reluctant to return to its scabbard. "You desire their gold. Is that why you aided me?"

The black-bearded soldier laughed. "I owed them a debt and had been biding my time, waiting to pay. These rascals are all that were left of a pirate crew which slew everyone aboard my own ship when we wandered into strange waters—they would have slain me had I not told them I wished to join them. Now I am revenged. Not that I am above taking the gold, since much of it belongs to me and my dead brothers. It will go to their wives and their children when I return to the Purple Towns."

"How did you convince them not to kill you, too?" Elric sought among the ruins of the fire for something to eat. He found some cheese and began to chew upon it.

"They had no captain or navigator, it seemed. None were real sailors at all, but coast-huggers, based upon this island. They were stranded here, you see, and had taken to piracy as a last resort, but were too terrified to risk the open sea. Besides, after the fight, they had no ship. We had managed to sink that as we fought. We sailed mine to this shore, but provisions were already low and they had no stomach for setting sail without full holds, so I pretended that I knew this coast (may the gods take my soul if I ever see it again after this business) and offered to lead them inland to a village they might loot. They had heard of no such village, but believed me when I said it lay in a hidden valley. That way I prolonged my life while I waited for the opportunity to be revenged upon them. It was a foolish hope, I know. Yet"—grinning—"as it happened, it was well-founded, after all! Eh?"

The black-bearded man glanced a little warily at Elric, uncertain of what the albino might say, hoping, however, for comradeship, though it was well known how haughty Melnibonéans were. Elric could tell that all these thoughts went through his new acquaintance's mind; he had seen many others make similar calculations. So he smiled openly and slapped the man on the shoulder.

"You saved my life, also, my friend. We are both fortunate."

The man sighed in relief and slung his ax upon his back. "Aye—lucky's the word. But shall our luck hold, I wonder?"

"You do not know the island at all?"

"Nor the waters, either. How we came to them I'll never guess. Enchanted waters, though, without question. You've seen the color of the sun?"

"I have."

"Well"—the seaman bent to remove a pendant from around the Pan Tangian's throat—"you'd know more about enchantments and sorceries than I. How came you here, Sir Melnibonéan?"

"I know not. I fled from some who hunted me. I came to a shore and could flee no further. Then I dreamed a great deal. When next I awoke I was on the shore again, but of this island."

"Spirits of some sort—maybe friendly to you—took you to safety, away from your enemies."

"That's just possible," Elric agreed, "for we have many allies among the elementals. I am called Elric and I am self-exiled from Melniboné. I travel because I believe I have something to learn from the folk of the Young Kingdoms. I have no power, save what you see. . . ."

The black-bearded man's eyes narrowed in appraisal as he pointed at himself with his thumb. "I'm Smiorgan Baldhead, once a sea-lord of the Purple Towns. I commanded a fleet of merchantmen. Perhaps I still do. I shall not know until I return—if I ever do return."

"Then let us pool our knowledge and our resources, Smiorgan Baldhead, and make plans to leave this island as soon as we can."

Elric walked back to where he saw traces of the abandoned game, trampled into the mud and the blood. From among the dice and the ivory slips, the silver and the bronze coins, he found the gold Melnibonéan wheel. He picked it up and held it in his outstretched palm. The wheel almost covered the whole palm. In the old days, it had been the currency of kings.

"This was yours, friend?" he asked Smiorgan.

Smiorgan Baldhead looked up from where he was still searching the Pan Tangian for his stolen possessions. He nodded.

"Aye. Would you keep it as part of your share?"

Elric shrugged. "I'd rather know from whence it came. Who gave it you?"

"It was not stolen. It's Melnibonéan, then?"

"Yes."

"I guessed it."

"From whom did you obtain it?"

Smiorgan straightened up, having completed his search. He scratched at a slight wound on his forearm. "It was used to buy passage on our ship—before we were lost— before the raiders attacked us."

"Passage? By a Melnibonéan?"

"Maybe," said Smiorgan. He seemed reluctant to speculate.

"Was he a warrior?"

Smiorgan smiled in his beard. "No. It was a woman gave that to me."

"How came she to take passage?"

Smiorgan began to pick up the rest of the money. "It's a long tale and, in part, a familiar one to most merchant sailors. We were seeking new markets for our goods and had equipped a good-sized fleet, which I commanded as the largest shareholder." He seated himself casually upon the big corpse of the Chalalite and began to count the money. "Would you hear the tale or do I bore you already?"

"I'd be glad to listen."

Reaching behind him, Smiorgan pulled a wine-flask from the belt of the corpse and offered it to Elric, who accepted it and drank sparingly of a wine which was unusually good.

Smiorgan took the flask when Elric had finished. "That's part of our cargo," he said. "We were proud of it. A good vintage, eh?"

"Excellent. So you set off from the Purple Towns?"

"Aye. Going east toward the Unknown Kingdoms. We sailed due east for a couple of weeks, sighting some of the bleakest coasts I have ever seen, and then we saw no land at all for another week. That was when we entered a stretch of water we came to call the Roaring Rocks—like the Serpent's Teeth off Shazar's coast, but much greater in expanse, and larger, too. Huge volcanic cliffs which rose from the sea on every side and around which the waters heaved and boiled and howled with a fierceness I've rarely experienced. Well, in short, the fleet was dispersed and at least four ships were lost on those rocks. At last we were able to escape those waters and found ourselves becalmed and alone. We searched for our sister ships for a while and then decided to give ourselves another week before turning for home, for we had no liking to go back into the Roaring Rocks again. Low on provisions, we sighted land at last—grassy cliffs and hospitable beaches and, inland, some signs of cultivation, so we knew we had found civilization again. We put into a small fishing port and satisfied the natives—who spoke no tongue used in the Young Kingdoms—that we were friendly. And that was when the woman approached us."

"The Melnibonéan woman?"

"If Melnibonéan she was. She was a fine-looking woman, I'll say that. We were short of provisions, as I told you, and short of any means of purchasing them, for the fishermen desired little of what we had to trade. Having given up our original quest, we were content to head westward again."

"The woman?"

"She wished to buy passage to the Young Kingdoms—and was content to go with us as far as Menii, our home port. For her passage she gave us two of those wheels. One was used to buy provisions in the town—Graghin, I think it was called—and after making repairs we set off again."

"You never reached the Purple Towns?"

"There were more storms—strange storms. Our instruments were useless, our lodestones were of no help to us at all. We became even more completely lost than before. Some of my men argued that we had gone beyond our own world altogether. Some blamed the woman, saying she was a sorceress who had no intention of going to Menii. But I believed her. Night fell and seemed to last forever until we sailed into a calm dawn beneath a blue sun. My men were close to panic—and it takes much to make my men panic—when we sighted the island. As we headed for it those pirates attacked us in a ship which belonged to history—it should have been on the bottom of the ocean, not on the surface. I've seen pictures of such craft in murals on a temple wall in Tarkesh. In ramming us, she stove in half her port side and was sinking even when they swarmed aboard. They were desperate, savage men, Elric—half-starved and blood-hungry. We were weary after our voyage, but fought well. During the fighting the woman disappeared, killed herself, maybe, when she saw the stamp of our conquerors. After a long fight only myself and one other, who died soon after, were left. That was when I became cunning and decided to wait for revenge."

"The woman had a name?"

"None she would give. I have thought the matter over and suspect that, after all, we were used by her. Perhaps she did not seek Menii and the Young Kingdoms. Perhaps it was this world she sought, and, by sorcery, led us here."

"This world? You think it different from our own?"

"If only because of the sun's strange color. Do you not

think so, too? You, with your Melnibonéan knowledge of such things, must believe it."

"I have dreamed of such things," Elric admitted, but he would say no more.

"Most of the pirates thought as I—they were from all the ages of the Young Kingdoms. That much I discovered. Some were from the earliest years of the era, some from our own time—and some were from the future. Adventurers, most of them, who, at some stage in their lives, sought a legendary land of great riches which lay on the other side of an ancient gateway, rising from the middle of the ocean; but they found themselves trapped here, unable to sail back through this mysterious gate. Others had been involved in sea-fights, thought themselves drowned and woken up on the shores of the island. Many, I suppose, had once had reasonable virtues, but there is little to support life on the island and they had become wolves, living off one another or any ship unfortunate enough to pass, inadvertently, through this gate of theirs."

Elric recalled part of his dream. "Did any call it the 'Crimson Gate'?"

"Several did, aye."

"And yet the theory is unlikely, if you'll forgive my skepticism," Elric said. "As one who has passed through the Shade Gate to Ameeron . . ."

"You know of other worlds, then?"

"I've never heard of this one. And I am versed in such matters. That is why I doubt the reasoning. And yet, there was the dream. . . ."

"Dream?"

"Oh, it was nothing. I am used to such dreams and give them no significance."

"The theory cannot seem surprising to a Melnibonéan, Elric!" Smiorgan grinned again. "It's I who should be skeptical, not you."

And Elric replied, half to himself: "Perhaps I fear the implications more." He lifted his head, and with the shaft of a broken spear, began to poke at the fire. "Certain ancient sorcerers of Melniboné proposed that an infinite number of worlds coexist with our own. Indeed, my

dreams, of late, have hinted as much!" He forced himself
to smile. "But I cannot afford to believe such things. Thus,
I reject them."

"Wait for the dawn," said Smiorgan Baldhead. "The
color of the sun shall prove the theory."

"Perhaps it will prove only that we both dream," said
Elric. The smell of death was strong in his nostrils. He
pushed aside those corpses nearest to the fire and settled himself to sleep.

Smiorgan Baldhead had begun to sing a strong yet lilting song in his own dialect, which Elrich could scarcely
follow.

"Do you sing of your victory over your enemies?" the
albino asked.

Smiorgan paused for a moment, half-amused. "No, Sir
Elric, I sing to keep the shades at bay. After all, these
fellows' ghosts must still be lurking nearby, in the dark,
so little time has passed since they died."

"Fear not," Elric told him. "Their souls are already
eaten."

But Smiorgan sang on, and his voice was louder, his
song more intense, than ever it had been before.

Just before he fell asleep, Elric thought he heard a horse
whinny, and he meant to ask Smiorgan if any of the pirates had been mounted, but he fell asleep before he
could do so.

Recalling little of his voyage on the Dark Ship, Elric
would never know how he came to reach the world in
which he now found himself. In later years he would recall most of these experiences as dreams, and indeed they
seemed dreamlike even as they occurred.

He slept uneasily, and in the morning the clouds were
heavier, shining with that strange, leaden light, though
the sun itself was obscured. Smiorgan Baldhead of the

Purple Towns was pointing upward, already on his feet, speaking with quiet triumph:

"Will that evidence suffice to convince you, Elric of Melniboné?"

"I am convinced of a quality about the light—possibly about this terrain—which makes the sun appear blue," Elric replied. He glanced with distaste around him at the carnage. The corpses made a wretched sight and he was filled with a nebulous misery that was neither remorse nor pity.

Smiorgan's sigh was sardonic. "Well, Sir Skeptic, we had best retrace my steps and seek my ship. What say you?"

"I agree," the albino told him.

"How far had you marched from the coast when you found us?"

Elric told him.

Smiorgan smiled. "You arrived in the nick of time, then. I should have been most embarrassed by today if the sea had been reached and I could show my pirate friends no village! I shall not forget this favor you have done me, Elric. I am a count of the Purple Towns and have much influence. If there is any service I can perform for you when we return, you must let me know."

"I thank you," Elric said gravely. "But first we must discover a means of escape."

Smiorgan had gathered up a satchel of food, some water and some wine. Elric had no stomach to make his breakfast among the dead, so he slung the satchel over his shoulder. "I'm ready," he said.

Smiorgan was satisfied. "Come—we go this way."

Elric began to follow the sea-lord over the dry, crunching turf. The steep sides of the valley loomed over them, tinged with a peculiar and unpleasant greenish hue, the result of the brown foliage being stained by the blue light from above. When they reached the river, which was narrow and ran rapidly through boulders giving easy means of crossing, they rested and ate. Both men were stiff from the previous night's fighting; both were glad to wash the dried blood and mud from their bodies in the water.

Refreshed, the pair climbed over the boulders and left the river behind, ascending the slopes, speaking little so that their breath was saved for the exertion. It was noon by the time they reached the top of the valley and observed a plain not unlike the one which Elric had first crossed. Elric now had a fair idea of the island's geography: it resembled the top of a mountain, with an indentation near the center which was the valley. Again he became sharply aware of the absence of any wildlife and remarked on this to Count Smiorgan, who agreed that he had seen nothing—no bird, fish, nor beast since he had arrived.

"It's a barren little world, friend Elric, and a misfortune for a mariner to be wrecked upon its shores."

They moved on, until the sea could be observed meeting the horizon in the far distance.

It was Elric who first heard the sound behind them, recognizing the steady thump of the hooves of a galloping horse, but when he looked back over his shoulder he could see no sign of a rider, nor anywhere that a rider could hide. He guessed that, in his tiredness, his ears were betraying him. It had been thunder that he had heard.

Smiorgan strode implacably onward, though he, too, must have heard the sound.

Again it came. Again, Elric turned. Again he saw nothing.

"Smiorgan? Did you hear a rider?"

Smiorgan continued to walk without looking back. "I heard," he grunted.

"You have heard it before?"

"Many times since I arrived. The pirates heard it, too, and some believed it their nemesis—an Angel of Death seeking them out for retribution."

"You don't know the source?"

Smiorgan paused, then stopped, and when he turned his face was grim. "Once or twice I have caught a glimpse of a horse, I think. A tall horse—white—richly dressed—but with no man upon his back. Ignore it, Elric, as I do.

We have larger mysteries with which to occupy our minds!"

"You are afraid of it, Smiorgan?"

He accepted this. "Aye. I confess it. But neither fear nor speculation will rid us of it. Come!"

Elric was bound to see the sense of Smiorgan's statement and he accepted it; yet when the sound came again, about an hour later, he could not resist turning. Then he thought he glimpsed the outline of a large stallion, caparisoned for riding, but that might have been nothing more than an idea Smiorgan had put in his mind.

The day grew colder and in the air was a peculiar, bitter odor. Elric remarked on the smell to Count Smiorgan and learned that this, too, was familiar.

"The smell comes and goes, but it is usually here in some strength."

"Like sulfur," said Elric.

Count Smiorgan's laugh had much irony in it, as if Elric made reference to some private joke of Smiorgan's own. "Oh, aye! Sulfur right enough!"

The drumming of hooves grew louder behind them as they neared the coast and at last Elric, and Smiorgan too, turned around again, to look.

And now a horse could be seen plainly—riderless, but saddled and bridled, its dark eyes intelligent, its beautiful white head held proudly.

"Are you still convinced of the absence of sorcery here, Sir Elric?" Count Smiorgan asked with some satisfaction. "The horse was invisible. Now it is visible." He shrugged the battle-ax on his shoulder into a better position. "Either that, or it moves from one world to another with ease, so that all we mainly hear are its hoofbeats."

"If so," said Elric sardonically, eyeing the stallion, "it might bear us back to our own world."

"You admit, then, that we are marooned in some Limbo?"

"Very well, yes. I admit the possibility."

"Have you no sorcery to trap the horse?"

"Sorcery does not come so easily to me, for I have no great liking for it," the albino told him.

As they spoke, they approached the horse, but it would let them get no closer. It snorted and moved backward, keeping the same distance between them and itself.

At last, Elric said, "We waste time, Count Smiorgan. Let's get to your ship with speed and forget blue suns and enchanted horses as quickly as we may. Once aboard the ship I can doubtless help you with a little incantation or two, for we'll need aid of some sort if we're to sail a large ship by ourselves."

They marched on, but the horse continued to follow them. They came to the edge of the cliffs, standing high above a narrow, rocky bay in which a battered ship lay at anchor. The ship had the high, fine lines of a Purple Towns merchantman, but its decks were piled with shreds of torn canvas, pieces of broken rope, shards of timber, torn-open bales of cloth, smashed wine-jars, and all manner of other refuse, while in several places her rails were smashed and two or three of her yards had splintered. It was evident that she had been through both storms and sea-fights and it was a wonder that she still floated.

"We'll have to tidy her up as best we can, using only the mains'l for motion," mused Smiorgan. "Hopefully we can salvage enough food to last us . . ."

"Look!" Elric pointed, sure that he had seen someone in the shadows near the afterdeck. "Did the pirates leave any of their company behind?"

"None."

"Did you see anyone on the ship, just then?"

"My eyes play filthy tricks on my mind," Smiorgan told him. "It is this damned blue light. There is a rat or two aboard, that's all. And that's what you saw."

"Possibly." Elric looked back. The horse appeared to be unaware of them as it cropped the brown grass. "Well, let's finish the journey."

They scrambled down the steeply sloping cliff-face and were soon on the shore, wading through the shallows for the ship, clambering up the slippery ropes which still hung over the sides, and, at last, setting their feet with some relief upon the deck.

"I feel more secure already," said Smiorgan. "This ship

was my home for so long!" He searched through the scattered cargo until he found an unbroken wine-jar, carved off the seal, and handed it to Elric. Elric lifted the heavy jar and let a little of the good wine flow into his mouth. As Count Smiorgan began to drink, Elric was sure he saw another movement near the afterdeck, and he moved closer.

Now he was certain that he heard strained, rapid breathing—like the breathing of one who sought to stifle his need for air rather than be detected. They were slight sounds, but the albino's ears, unlike his eyes, were sharp. His hand ready to draw his sword, he stalked toward the source of the sound, Smiorgan now behind him.

She emerged from her hiding place before he reached her. Her hair hung in heavy, dirty coils about her pale face; her shoulders were slumped and her soft arms hung limply at her sides, and her dress was stained and ripped.

As Elric approached, she fell on her knees before him. "Take my life," she said humbly, "but I beg you—do not take me back to Saxif D'Aan, though I know you must be his servant or his kinsman."

"It's she!" cried Smiorgan in astonishment. "It's our passenger. She must have been in hiding all this time."

Elric stepped forward, lifting up the girl's chin so that he could study her face. There was a Melnibonéan cast about her features, but she was, to his mind, of the Young Kingdoms; she lacked the pride of a Melnibonéan woman, too. "What name was that you used, girl?" he asked kindly. "Did you speak of Saxif D'Aan? Earl Saxif D'Aan of Melniboné?"

"I did, my lord."

"Do not fear me as his servant," Elric told her. "And as for being a kinsman, I suppose you could call me that, on my mother's side—or rather my great-grandmother's side. He was an ancestor. He must have been dead for two centuries, at least!"

"No," she said. "He lives, my lord."

"On this island?"

"This island is not his home, but it is in this plane that

he exists. I sought to escape him through the Crimson
Gate. I fled through the gate in a skiff, reached the town
where you found me, Count Smiorgan, but he drew me
back once I was aboard your ship. He drew me back and
the ship with me. For that, I have remorse—and for what
befell your crew. Now I know he seeks me. I can feel his
presence growing nearer."

"Is he invisible?" Smiorgan asked suddenly. "Does he
ride a white horse?"

She gasped. "You see! He *is* near! Why else should the
horse appear on this island?"

"He rides it?" Elric asked.

"No, no! He fears the horse almost as much as I fear
him. The horse pursues him!"

Elric produced the Melnibonéan gold wheel from his
purse. "Did you take this from Earl Saxif D'Aan?"

"I did."

The albino frowned.

"Who is this man, Elric?" Count Smiorgan asked.
"You describe him as an ancestor—yet he lives in this
world. What do you know of him?"

Elric weighed the large gold wheel in his hand before
replacing it in his pouch. "He was something of a legend in Melniboné. His story is part of our literature. He
was a great sorcerer—one of the greatest—and he fell in
love. It's rare enough for Melnibonéans to fall in love, as
others understand the emotion, but rarer for one to have
such feelings for a girl who was not even of our own
race. She was half-Melnibonéan, so I heard, but from a
land which was, in those days, a Melnibonéan possession,
a western province close to Dharijor. She was bought by
him in a batch of slaves he planned to use for some sorcerous experiment, but he singled her out, saving her from
whatever fate it was the others suffered. He lavished his
attention upon her, giving her everything. For her, he
abandoned his practices, retired to live quietly away from
Imrryr, and I think she showed him a certain affection,
though she did not seem to love him. There was another,
you see, called Carolak, as I recall, and also half-Melnibonéan, who had become a mercenary in Shazar and risen

in the favor of the Shazarian court. She had been pledged to this Carolak before her abduction. . . ."

"She loved him?" Count Smiorgan asked.

"She was pledged to marry him, but let me finish my story. . . ." Elric continued: "Well, at length Carolak, now a man of some substance, second only to the king in Shazar, heard of her fate and swore to rescue her. He came with raiders to Melniboné's shores, and aided by sorcery, sought out Saxif D'Aan's palace. That done, he sought the girl, finding her at last in the apartments Saxif D'Aan had set aside for her use. He told her that he had come to claim her as his bride, to rescue her from persecution. Oddly, the girl resisted, suggesting that she had been too long a slave in the Melnibonéan harem to readapt to the life of a princess in the Shazarian court. Carolak scoffed at this and seized her. He managed to escape the castle and had the girl over the saddle of his horse and was about to rejoin his men on the coast when Saxif D'Aan detected them. Carolak, I think, was slain, or else a spell was put on him, but Saxif D'Aan, in his terrible jealousy and certain that the girl had planned the escape with a lover, ordered her to die upon the Wheel of Chaos—a machine rather like that coin in design. Her limbs were broken slowly and Saxif D'Aan sat and watched, through long days, while she died. Her skin was peeled from her flesh, and Earl Saxif D'Aan observed every detail of her punishment. Soon it was evident that the drugs and sorcery used to sustain her life were failing and Saxif D'Aan ordered her taken from the Wheel of Chaos and laid upon a couch. 'Well,' he said, 'you have been punished for betraying me and I am glad. Now you may die.' And he saw that her lips, blood-caked and frightful, were moving, and he bent to hear her words."

"Those words? Revenge? An oath?" asked Smiorgan.

"Her last gesture was an attempt to embrace him. And the words were those she had never uttered to him before, much as he had hoped that she would. She said simply, over and over again, until the last breath left her: 'I love you. I love you. I love you.' And then she died."

Smiorgan rubbed at his beard. "Gods! What then? What did your ancestor do?"

"He knew remorse."

"Of course!"

"Not so, for a Melnibonéan. Remorse is a rare emotion with us. Few have ever experienced it. Torn by guilt, Earl Saxif D'Aan left Melniboné, never to return. It was assumed that he had died in some remote land, trying to make amends for what he had done to the only creature he had ever loved. But now, it seems, he sought the Crimson Gate, perhaps thinking it an opening into Hell."

"But why should he plague me!" the girl cried. "I am not she! My name is Vassliss. I am a merchant's daughter, from Jharkor. I was voyaging to visit my uncle in Vilmir when our ship was wrecked. A few of us escaped in an open boat. More storms seized us. I was flung from the boat and was drowning when"—she shuddered—"when *his* galley found me. I was grateful, then . . ."

"What happened?" Elric pushed the matted hair away from her face and offered her some of their wine. She drank gratefully.

"He took me to his palace and told me that he would marry me, that I should be his empress forever and rule beside him. But I was frightened. There was such pain in him—and such cruelty, too. I thought he must devour me, destroy me. Soon after my capture, I took the money and the boat and fled for the gateway, which he had told me about. . . ."

"You could find this gateway for us?" Elric asked.

"I think so. I have some knowledge of seamanship, learned from my father. But what would be the use, sir? He would find us again and drag us back. And he must be very near, even now."

"I have a little sorcery myself," Elric assured her, "and will pit it against Saxif D'Aan's, if I must." He turned to Count Smiorgan. "Can we get a sail aloft quickly?"

"Fairly quickly."

"Then let's hurry, Count Smiorgan Baldhead. I might have the means of getting us through this Crimson Gate and free from any further involvement in the dealings of the dead!"

IV

While Count Smiorgan and Vassliss of Jharkor watched, Elric lowered himself to the deck, panting and pale. His first attempt to work sorcery in this world had failed and had exhausted him.

"I am further convinced," he told Smiorgan, "that we are in another plane of existence, for I should have worked my incantations with less effort."

"You have failed."

Elric rose with some difficulty. "I shall try again."

He turned his white face skyward; he closed his eyes; he stretched out his arms and his body tensed as he began the incantation again, his voice growing louder and louder, higher and higher, so that it resembled the shrieking of a gale.

He forgot where he was; he forgot his own identity; he forgot those who were with him as his whole mind concentrated upon the summoning. He sent his call out beyond the confines of the world, into that strange plane where the elementals dwelled—where the powerful creatures of the air could still be found—the *sylphs* of the breeze, and the *sharnahs*, who lived in the storms, and the most powerful of all, the *h'Haarshanns,* creatures of the whirlwind.

And now at last some of them began to come at his summons, ready to serve him as, by virtue of an ancient pact, the elementals had served his forefathers. And slowly the sail of the ship began to fill, and the timbers creaked, and Smiorgan raised the anchor, and the ship was sailing away from the island, through the rocky gap of the harbor, and out into the open sea, still beneath a strange blue sun.

Soon a huge wave was forming around them, lifting

up the ship and carrying it across the ocean, so that
Count Smiorgan and the girl marveled at the speed of
their progress, while Elric, his crimson eyes open now,
but blank and unseeing, continued to croon to his unseen
allies.

Thus the ship progressed across the waters of the sea,
and at last the island was out of sight and the girl, check-
ing their position against the position of the sun, was able
to give Count Smiorgan sufficient information for him to
steer a course.

As soon as he could, Count Smiorgan went up to Elric,
who still straddled the deck, still as stiff-limbed as before,
and shook him.

"Elric! You will kill yourself with this effort. We need
your friends no longer!"

At once the wind dropped and the wave dispersed and
Elric, gasping, fell to the deck.

"It is harder here," he said. "It is so much harder
here. It is as if I have to call across far greater gulfs than
any I have known before."

And then Elric slept.

He lay in a warm bunk in a cool cabin. Through the
porthole filtered diffused blue light. He sniffed. He caught
the odor of hot food, and turning his head, saw that Vassliss stood there, a bowl of broth in her hands. "I was able
to cook this," she said. "It will improve your health. As
far as I can tell, we are nearing the Crimson Gate. The
seas are always rough around the gate, so you will need
your strength."

Elric thanked her pleasantly and began to eat the broth
as she watched him.

"You are very like Saxif D'Aan," she said. "Yet harder
in a way—and gentler, too. He is so remote. I know why
that girl could never tell him that she loved him."

Elric smiled. "Oh, it's nothing more than a folktale,
probably, the story I told you. This Saxif D'Aan could
be another person altogether—or an impostor, even, who
has taken his name—or a sorcerer. Some sorcerers take

the names of other sorcerers, for they think it gives them more power."

There came a cry from above, but Elric could not make out the words.

The girl's expression became alarmed. Without a word to Elric, she hurried from the cabin.

Elric, rising unsteadily, followed her up the companionway.

Count Smiorgan Baldhead was at the wheel of his ship and he was pointing toward the horizon behind them. "What do you make of that, Elric?"

Elric peered at the horizon, but could see nothing. Often his eyes were weak, as now. But the girl said in a voice of quiet despair:

"It is a golden sail."

"You recognize it?" Elric asked her.

"Oh, indeed I do. It is the galleon of Earl Saxif D'Aan. He has found us. Perhaps he was lying in wait along our route, knowing we must come this way."

"How far are we from the gate?"

"I am not sure."

At that moment, there came a terrible noise from below, as if something sought to stave in the timbers of the ship.

"It's in the forward hatches!" cried Smiorgan. "See what it is, friend Elric! But take care, man!"

Cautiously Elric prised back one of the hatch covers and peered into the murky fastness of the hold. The noise of stamping and thumping continued on, and as his eyes adjusted to the light, he saw the source.

The white horse was there. It whinnied as it saw him, almost in greeting.

"How did it come aboard?" Elric asked. "I saw nothing. I heard nothing."

The girl was almost as white as Elric. She sank to her knees beside the hatch, burying her face in her arms.

"He has us! He has us!"

"There is still a chance we can reach the Crimson Gate in time," Elric reassured her. "And once in my own world, why, I can work much stronger sorcery to protect us."

"No," she sobbed, "it is too late. Why else would the white horse be here? He knows that Saxif D'Aan must soon board us."

"He'll have to fight us before he shall have you," Elric promised her.

"You have not seen his men. Cutthroats all. Desperate and wolfish! They'll show you no mercy. You would be best advised to hand me over to Saxif D'Aan at once and save yourselves. You'll gain nothing from trying to protect me. But I'd ask you a favor."

"What's that?"

"Find me a small knife to carry, that I may kill myself as soon as I know you two are safe."

Elric laughed, dragging her to her feet. "I'll have no such melodramatics from you, lass! We stand together. Perhaps we can bargain with Saxif D'Aan."

"What have you to barter?"

"Very little. But he is not aware of that."

"He can read your thoughts, seemingly. He has great powers!"

"I am Elric of Melniboné. I am said to possess a certain facility in the sorcerous arts, myself."

"But you are not as single-minded as Saxif D'Aan," she said simply. "Only one thing obsesses him—the need to make me his consort."

"Many girls would be flattered by the attention—glad to be an empress with a Melnibonéan emperor for a husband." Elric was sardonic.

She ignored his tone. "That is why I fear him so," she said in a murmur. "If I lost my determination for a moment, I could love him. I should be destroyed! It is what *she* must have known!"

V

The gleaming galleon, sails and sides all gilded so that it seemed the sun itself pursued them, moved rapidly upon them while the girl and Count Smiorgan watched aghast and Elric desperately attempted to recall his elemental allies, without success.

Through the pale blue light the golden ship sailed relentlessly in their wake. Its proportions were monstrous, its sense of power vast, its gigantic prow sending up huge, foamy waves on both sides as it sped silently toward them.

With the look of a man preparing himself to meet death, Count Smiorgan Baldhead of the Purple Towns unslung his battle-ax and loosened his sword in its scabbard, setting his little metal cap upon his bald pate. The girl made no sound, no movement at all, but she wept.

Elric shook his head and his long, milk-white hair formed a halo around his face for a moment. His moody crimson eyes began to focus on the world around him. He recognized the ship; it was of a pattern with the golden battle-barges of Melniboné—doubtless the ship in which Earl Saxif D'Aan had fled his homeland, searching for the Crimson Gate. Now Elric was convinced that this must be that same Saxif D'Aan and he knew less fear than did his companions, but considerably greater curiosity. Indeed, it was almost with nostalgia that he noted the ball of fire, like a natural comet, glowing with green light, come hissing and spluttering toward them, flung by the ship's forward catapult. He half expected to see a great dragon wheeling in the sky overhead, for it was with dragons and gilded battle-craft like these that Melniboné had once conquered the world.

The fireball fell into the sea a few inches from their bow and was evidently placed there deliberately, as a warning.

"Don't stop!" cried Vassliss. "Let the flames slay us! It will be better!"

Smiorgan was looking upward. "We have no choice. Look! He has banished the wind, it seems."

They were becalmed. Elric smiled a grim smile. He knew now what the folk of the Young Kingdoms must have felt when his ancestors had used these identical tactics against them.

"Elric?" Smiorgan turned to the albino. "Are these your people? That ship's Melnibonéan without question!"

"So are the methods," Elric told him. "I am of the blood royal of Melniboné. I could be emperor, even now, if I chose to claim my throne. There is some small chance that Earl Saxif D'Aan, though an ancestor, will recognize me and, therefore, recognize my authority. We are a conservative people, the folk of the Dragon Isle."

The girl spoke through dry lips, hopelessly: "He recognizes only the authority of the Lords of Chaos, who give him aid."

"All Melnibonéans recognize that authority," Elric told her with a certain humor.

From the forward hatch, the sound of the stallion's stamping and snorting increased.

"We're besieged by enchantments!" Count Smiorgan's normally ruddy features had paled. "Have you none of your own, Prince Elric, you can use to counter them?"

"None, it seems."

The golden ship loomed over them. Elric saw that the rails, high overhead, were crowded not with Imrryrian warriors but with cutthroats equally as desperate as those he had fought upon the island, and, apparently, drawn from the same variety of historical periods and nations. The galleon's long sweeps scraped the sides of the smaller vessel as they folded, like the legs of some water insect, to enable the grappling irons to be flung out. Iron claws bit into the timbers of the little ship and the brigandly crowd overhead cheered, grinning at them, menacing them with their weapons.

The girl began to run to the seaward side of the ship, but Elric caught her by the arm.

"Do not stop me, I beg you!" she cried. "Rather, jump with me and drown!"

"You think that death will save you from Saxif D'Aan?" Elric said. "If he has the power you say, death will only bring you more firmly into his grasp!"

"Oh!" The girl shuddered and then, as a voice called down to them from one of the tall decks of the gilded ship, she gave a moan and fainted into Elric's arms, so that, weakened as he was by his spell-working, it was all that he could do to stop himself falling with her to the deck.

The voice rose over the coarse shouts and guffaws of the crew. It was pure, lilting, and sardonic. It was the voice of a Melnibonéan, though it spoke the common tongue of the Young Kingdoms, a corruption, in itself, of the speech of the Bright Empire.

"May I have the captain's permission to come aboard?"

Count Smiorgan growled back: "You have us firm, sir! Don't try to disguise an act of piracy with a polite speech!"

"I take it I have your permission, then." The unseen speaker's tone remained exactly the same.

Elric watched as part of the rail was drawn back to allow a gangplank, studded with golden nails to give firmer footing, to be lowered from the galleon's deck to theirs.

A tall figure appeared at the top of the gangplank. He had the fine features of a Melnibonéan nobleman, was thin, proud in his bearing, clad in voluminous robes of cloth-of-gold, an elaborate helmet in gold and ebony upon his long auburn locks. He had gray-blue eyes, pale, slightly flushed skin, and he carried, so far as Elric could see, no weapons of any kind.

With considerable dignity, Earl Saxif D'Aan began to descend, his rascals at his back. The contrast between this beautiful intellectual and those he commanded was remarkable. Where he walked with straight back, elegant and noble, they slouched, filthy, degenerate, unintelligent, grinning with pleasure at their easy victory. Not a man among them showed any sign of human dignity; each was overdressed in tattered and unclean finery, each had at least three weapons upon his person, and there was much evidence of looted jewelry, of nose-rings, earrings, bangles, necklaces, toe- and finger-rings, pendants, cloak-pins, and the like.

"Gods!" murmured Smiorgan. "I've rarely seen such a collection of scum, and I thought I'd encountered most kinds in my voyages. How can such a man bear to be in their company?"

"Perhaps it suits his sense of irony," Elric suggested.

Earl Saxif D'Aan reached their deck and stood looking up at them to where they still positioned themselves, in the poop. He gave a slight bow. His features were controlled and only his eyes suggested something of the intensity of emotion dwelling within him, particularly as they fell upon the girl in Elric's arms.

"I am Earl Saxif D'Aan of Melniboné, now of the Islands Beyond the Crimson Gate. You have something with you which is mine. I would claim it from you."

"You mean the Lady Vassliss of Jharkor?" Elric said, his voice as steady as Saxif D'Aan's.

Saxif D'Aan seemed to note Elric for the first time. A slight frown crossed his brow and was quickly dismissed. "She is mine," he said. "You may be assured that she will come to no harm at my hands."

Elric, seeking some advantage, knew that he risked much when he next spoke, in the High Tongue of Melniboné, used between those of the blood royal. "Knowledge of your history does not reassure me, Saxif D'Aan."

Almost imperceptibly, the golden man stiffened and fire flared in his gray-blue eyes. "Who are you, to speak the Tongue of Kings? Who are you, who claims knowledge of my past?"

"I am Elric, son of Sadric, and I am the four-hundred-and-twenty-eighth emperor of the folk of R'lin K'ren A'a, who landed upon the Dragon Isle ten thousand years ago. I am Elric, your emperor, Earl Saxif D'Aan, and I demand your fealty." And Elric held up his right hand, upon which still gleamed a ring set with a single Actorios stone, the Ring of Kings.

Earl Saxif D'Aan now had firm control of himself

again. He gave no sign that he was impressed. "Your sovereignty does not extend beyond your own world, noble emperor, though I greet you as a fellow monarch." He spread his arms so that his long sleeves rustled. "This world is mine. All that exists beneath the blue sun do I rule. You trespass, therefore, in my domain. I have every right to do as I please."

"Pirate pomp," muttered Count Smiorgan, who had understood nothing of the conversation but had gathered something of what passed by the tone. "Pirate braggadocio. What does he say, Elric?"

"He convinces me that he is not, in your sense, a pirate, Count Smiorgan. He claims that he is ruler of this plane. Since there is apparently no other, we must accept his claim."

"Gods! Then let him behave like a monarch and let us sail safely out of his waters!"

"We may—if we give him the girl."

Count Smiorgan shook his head. "I'll not do that. She's my passenger, in my charge. I must die rather than do that. It is the Code of the Sea-lords of the Purple Towns."

"You are famous for your adherence to that code," Elric said. "As for myself, I have taken this girl into my protection and, as hereditary emperor of Melniboné, I cannot allow myself to be browbeaten."

They had conversed in a murmur, but, somehow, Earl Saxif D'Aan had heard them.

"I must let you know," he said evenly, in the common tongue, "that the girl is mine. You steal her from me. Is that the action of an emperor?"

"She is not a slave," Elric said, "but the daughter of a free merchant in Jharkor. You have no rights upon her."

Earl Saxif D'Aan said, "Then I cannot open the Crimson Gate for you. You must remain in my world forever."

"You have closed the gate? Is it possible?"

"To me."

"Do you know that the girl would rather die than be captured by you, Earl Saxif D'Aan? Does it give you pleasure to instill such fear?"

The golden man looked directly into Elric's eyes as if

he made some cryptic challenge. "The gift of pain has ever been a favorite gift among our folk, has it not? Yet it is another gift I offer her. She calls herself Vassliss of Jharkor, but she does not know herself. I know her. She is Gratyesha, Princess of Fwem-Omeyo, and I would make her my bride."

"How can it be that she does not know her own name?"

"She is reincarnated—soul and flesh are identical—that is how I know. And I have waited, Emperor of Melniboné, for many scores of years for her. Now I shall not be cheated of her."

"As you cheated yourself, two centuries past, in Melniboné?"

"You risk much with your directness of language, brother monarch!" There was a hint of a warning in Saxif D'Aan's tone, a warning much fiercer than any implied by the words.

"Well"—Elric shrugged—"you have more power than we do. My sorcery works poorly in your world. Your ruffians outnumber us. It should not be difficult for you to take her from us."

"You must give her to me. Then you may go free, back to your own world and your own time."

Elric smiled. "There is sorcery here. She is no reincarnation. You'd bring your lost love's spirit from the netherworld to inhabit this girl's body. Am I not right? That is why she must be given freely, or your sorcery will rebound upon you—or might—and you would not take the risk."

Earl Saxif D'Aan turned his head away so that Elric might not see his eyes. "She is the girl," he said, in the High Tongue. "I know that she is. I mean her soul no harm. I would merely give it back its memory."

"Then it is stalemate," said Elric.

"Have you no loyalty to a brother of the royal blood?" Saxif D'Aan murmured, still refusing to look at Elric.

"You claimed no such loyalty, as I recall, Earl Saxif D'Aan. If you accept me as your emperor, then you must accept my decisions. I keep the girl in my custody. Or you must take her by force."

"I am too proud."

"Such pride shall ever destroy love," said Elric, almost in sympathy. "What now, King of Limbo? What shall you do with us?"

Earl Saxif D'Aan lifted his noble head, about to reply, when from the hold the stamping and the snorting began again. His eyes widened. He looked questioningly at Elric, and there was something close to terror in his face.

"What's that? What have you in the hold?"

"A mount, my lord, that is all," said Elric equably.

"A horse? An ordinary horse?"

"A white one. A stallion, with bridle and saddle. It has no rider."

At once Saxif D'Aan's voice rose as he shouted orders for his men. "Take those three aboard our ship. This one shall be sunk directly. Hurry! Hurry!"

Elric and Smiorgan shook off the hands which sought to seize them and they moved toward the gangplank, carrying the girl between them, while Smiorgan muttered, "At least we are not slain, Elric. But what becomes of us now?"

Elric shook his head. "We must hope that we can continue to use Earl Saxif D'Aan's pride against him, to our advantage, though the gods alone know how we shall resolve the dilemma."

Earl Saxif D'Aan was already hurrying up the gangplank ahead of them.

"Quickly," he shouted. "Raise the plank!"

They stood upon the decks of the golden battle-barge and watched as the gangplank was drawn up, the length of rail replaced.

"Bring up the catapults," Saxif D'Aan commanded. "Use lead. Sink that vessel at once!"

The noise from the forward hold increased. The horse's voice echoed over ships and water. Hooves smashed at timber and then, suddenly, it came crashing through the hatch-covers, scrambling for purchase on the deck with its front hooves, and then standing there, pawing at the planks, its neck arching, its nostrils dilating, and its eyes glaring, as if ready to do battle.

Now Saxif D'Aan made no attempt to hide the terror on his face. His voice rose to a scream as he threatened his rascals with every sort of horror if they did not obey him with utmost speed. The catapults were dragged up and huge globes of lead were lobbed onto the decks of Smiorgan's ship, smashing through the planks like arrows through parchment so that almost immediately the ship began to sink.

"Cut the grappling hooks!" cried Saxif D'Aan, wrenching a blade from the hand of one of his men and sawing at the nearest rope. "Cast loose—quickly!"

Even as Smiorgan's ship groaned and roared like a drowning beast, the ropes were cut. The ship keeled over at once, and the horse disappeared.

"Turn about!" shouted Saxif D'Aan. "Back to Fhaligarn and swiftly, or your souls shall feed my fiercest demons!"

There came a peculiar, high-pitched neighing from the foaming water, as Smiorgan's ship, stern uppermost, gasped and was swallowed. Elric caught a glimpse of the white stallion, swimming strongly.

"Go below!" Saxif D'Aan ordered, indicating a hatchway. "The horse can smell the girl and thus is doubly difficult to lose."

"Why do you fear it?" Elric asked. "It is only a horse. It cannot harm you."

Saxif D'Aan uttered a laugh of profound bitterness. "Can it not, brother monarch? Can it not?"

As they carried the girl below, Elric was frowning, remembering a little more of the legend of Saxif D'Aan, of the girl he had punished so cruelly, and of her lover, Prince Carolak. The last he heard of Saxif D'Aan was the sorcerer crying:

"More sail! More sail!"

And then the hatch had closed behind them and they found themselves in an opulent Melnibonéan day-cabin, full of rich hangings, precious metal, decorations of exquisite beauty and, to Count Smiorgan, disturbing decadence. But it was Elric, as he lowered the girl to a couch, who noticed the smell.

"Augh! It's the smell of a tomb—of damp and mold. Yet nothing rots. It is passing peculiar, friend Smiorgan, is it not?"

"I scarcely noticed, Elric." Smiorgan's voice was hollow. "But I would agree with you on one thing. We are entombed. I doubt we'll live to escape this world now."

VI

An hour had passed since they had been forced aboard. The door had been locked behind them, and it seemed Saxif D'Aan was too preoccupied with escaping the white stallion to bother with them. Peering through the lattice of a porthole, Elric could look back to where their ship had been sunk. They were many leagues distant already; yet he still thought, from time to time, that he saw the head and shoulders of the stallion above the waves.

Vassliss had recovered and sat pale and shivering upon the couch.

"What more do you know of that horse?" Elric asked her. "It would be helpful to me if you could recall anything you have heard."

She shook her head. "Saxif D'Aan spoke little of it, but I gather he fears the rider more than he does the horse."

"Ah!" Elric frowned. "I suspected it! Have you ever seen the rider?"

"Never. I think that Saxif D'Aan has never seen him, either. I think he believes himself doomed if that rider should ever sit upon the white stallion."

Elric smiled to himself.

"Why do you ask so much about the horse?" Smiorgan wished to know.

Elric shook his head. "I have an instinct, that is all. Half a memory. But I'll say nothing and think as little as I may, for there is no doubt Saxif D'Aan, as Vassliss suggests, has some power of reading the mind."

They heard a footfall above, descending to their door.

A bolt was drawn and Saxif D'Aan, his composure fully restored, stood in the opening, his hands in his golden sleeves.

"You will forgive, I hope, the peremptory way in which I sent you here. There was danger which had to be averted at all costs. As a result, my manners were not all that they should have been."

"Danger to us?" Elric asked. "Or to you, Earl Saxif D'Aan?"

"In the circumstances, to all of us, I assure you."

"Who rides the horse?" Smiorgan asked bluntly. "And why do you fear him?"

Earl Saxif D'Aan was master of himself again, so there was no sign of a reaction. "That is very much my private concern," he said softly. "Will you dine with me now?"

The girl made a noise in her throat and Earl Saxif D'Aan turned piercing eyes upon her. "Gratyesha, you will want to cleanse yourself and make yourself beautiful again. I will see that facilities are placed at your disposal."

"I am not Gratyesha," she said. "I am Vassliss, the merchant's daughter."

"You will remember," he said. "In time, you will remember." There was such certainty, such obsessive power, in his voice that even Elric experienced a frisson of awe. "The things will be brought to you, and you may use this cabin as your own until we return to my palace on Fhaligarn. My lords . . ." He indicated that they should leave.

Elric said, "I'll not leave her, Saxif D'Aan. She is too afraid."

"She fears only the truth, brother."

"She fears you and your madness."

Saxif D'Aan shrugged insouciantly. "I shall leave first, then. If you would accompany me, my lords . . ." He strode from the cabin and they followed.

Elric said, over his shoulder, "Vassliss, you may depend upon my protection." And he closed the cabin doors behind him.

Earl Saxif D'Aan was standing upon the deck, exposing his noble face to the spray which was flung up by the ship as it moved with supernatural speed through the sea.

"You called me mad, Prince Elric? Yet you must be versed in sorcery, yourself."

"Of course. I am of the blood royal. I am reckoned knowledgeable in my own world."

"But here? How well does your sorcery work?"

"Poorly, I'll admit. The spaces between the planes seem greater."

"Exactly. But I have bridged them. I have time to learn how to bridge them."

"You are saying that you are more powerful than am I?"

"It is a fact, is it not?"

"It is. But I did not think we were about to indulge in sorcerous battles, Earl Saxif D'Aan."

"Of course. Yet, if you were to think of besting me by sorcery, you would think twice, eh?"

"I should be foolish to contemplate such a thing at all. It could cost me my soul. My life, at least."

"True. You are a realist, I see."

"I suppose so."

"Then we can progress on simpler lines, to settle the dispute between us."

"You propose a duel?" Elric was surprised.

Earl Saxif D'Aan's laughter was light. "Of course not—against your sword? That has power in all worlds, though the magnitude varies."

"I'm glad that you are aware of that," Elric said significantly.

"Besides," added Earl Saxif D'Aan, his golden robes rustling as he moved a little nearer to the rail, "you would not kill me—for only I have the means of your escaping this world."

"Perhaps we'd elect to remain," said Elric.

"Then you would be my subjects. But, no—you would not like it here. I am self-exiled. I could not return to my own world now, even if I wished to do so. It has cost me much, my knowledge. But I would found a dynasty here, beneath the blue sun. I must have my wife, Prince Elric. I must have Gratyesha."

"Her name is Vassliss," said Elric obstinately.

"She thinks it is."

"Then it is. I have sworn to protect her, as has Count Smiorgan. Protect her we shall. You will have to kill us all."

"Exactly," said Earl Saxif D'Aan with the air of a man who has been coaching a poor student toward the correct answer to a problem. "Exactly. I shall have to kill you all. You leave me with little alternative, Prince Elric."

"Would that benefit you?"

"It would. It would put a certain powerful demon at my service for a few hours."

"We should resist."

"I have many men. I do not value them. Eventually, they would overwhelm you. Would they not?"

Elric remained silent.

"My men would be aided by sorcery," added Saxif D'Aan. "Some would die, but not too many, I think."

Elric was looking beyond Saxif D'Aan, staring out to sea. He was sure that the horse still followed. He was sure that Saxif D'Aan knew, also.

"And if we gave up the girl?"

"I should open the Crimson Gate for you. You would be honored guests. I should see that you were borne safely through, even taken safely to some hospitable land in your own world, for even if you passed through the gate there would be danger. The storms."

Elric appeared to deliberate.

"You have only a little time to make your decision, Prince Elric. I had hoped to reach my palace, Fhaligarn, by now. I shall not allow you very much longer. Come, make your decision. You know I speak the truth."

"You know that I can work some sorcery in your world, do you not?"

"You summoned a few friendly elementals to your aid, I know. But at what cost? Would you challenge me directly?"

"It would be unwise of me," said Elric.

Smiorgan was tugging at his sleeve. "Stop this useless

talk. He knows that we have given our word to the girl and that we *must* fight him!"

Earl Saxif D'Aan sighed. There seemed to be genuine sorrow in his voice. "If you are determined to lose your lives . . ." he began.

"I should like to know why you set such importance upon the speed with which we make up our minds," Elric said. "Why cannot we wait until we reach Fhaligarn?"

Earl Saxif D'Aan's expression was calculating, and again he looked full into Elric's crimson eyes. "I think you know," he said, almost inaudibly.

But Elric shook his head. "I think you give me too much credit for intelligence."

"Perhaps."

Elric knew that Saxif D'Aan was attempting to read his thoughts; he deliberately blanked his mind, and suspected that he sensed frustration in the sorcerer's demeanor.

And then the albino had sprung at his kinsman, his hand chopping at Saxif D'Aan's throat. The earl was taken completely off guard. He tried to call out, but his vocal chords were numbed. Another blow, and he fell to the deck, senseless.

"Quickly, Smiorgan," Elric shouted, and he had leaped into the rigging, climbing swiftly upward to the top yards. Smiorgan, bewildered, followed, and Elric had drawn his sword, even as he reached the crow's nest, driving upward through the rail so that the lookout was taken in the groin scarcely before he realized it.

Next, Elric was hacking at the ropes holding the mainsail to the yard. Already a number of Saxif D'Aan's ruffians were climbing after them.

The heavy golden sail came loose, falling to envelop the pirates and take several of them down with it.

Elric climbed into the crow's nest and pitched the dead man over the rail in the wake of his comrades. Then he had raised his sword over his head, holding it in his two hands, his eyes blank again, his head raised to the blue sun, and Smiorgan, clinging to the mast below, shuddered as he heard a peculiar crooning come from the albino's throat.

More of the cutthroats were ascending, and Smiorgan hacked at the rigging, having the satisfaction of seeing half a score go flying down to break their bones on the deck below, or be swallowed by the waves.

Earl Saxif D'Aan was beginning to recover, but he was still stunned.

"Fool!" he was crying. "Fool!" But it was not possible to tell if he referred to Elric or to himself.

Elric's voice became a wail, rhythmical and chilling, as he chanted his incantation, and the strength from the man he had killed flowed into him and sustained him. His crimson eyes seemed to flicker with fires of another, nameless color, and his whole body shook as the strange runes shaped themselves in a throat which had never been made to speak such sounds.

His voice became a vibrant groan as the incantation continued, and Smiorgan, watching as more of the crew made efforts to climb the mainmast, felt an unearthly coldness creep through him.

Earl Saxif D'Aan screamed from below:

"You would not dare!"

The sorcerer began to make passes in the air, his own incantation tumbling from his lips, and Smiorgan gasped as a creature made of smoke took shape only a few feet below him. The creature smacked its lips and grinned and stretched a paw, which became flesh even as it moved, toward Smiorgan. He hacked at the paw with his sword, whimpering.

"Elric!" cried Count Smiorgan, clambering higher so that he grasped the rail of the crow's nest. "Elric! He sends demons against us now!"

But Elric ignored him. His whole mind was in another world, a darker, bleaker world even than this one. Through gray mists, he saw a figure, and he cried a name. "Come!" he called in the ancient tongue of his ancestors. "Come!"

Count Smiorgan cursed as the demon became increasingly substantial. Red fangs clashed and green eyes glared

at him. A claw stroked his boot and no matter how much
he struck with his sword, the demon did not appear to
notice the blows.

There was no room for Smiorgan in the crow's nest, but
he stood on the outer rim, shouting with terror, desperate for aid. Still Elric continued to chant.

"Elric! I am doomed!"

The demon's paw grasped Smiorgan by his ankle.

"Elric!"

Thunder rolled out at sea; a bolt of lightning appeared
for a second and then was gone. From nowhere there
came the sound of a horse's hooves pounding, and a human voice shouting in triumph.

Elric sank back against the rail, opening his eyes in
time to see Smiorgan being dragged slowly downward.
With the last of his strength he flung himself forward,
leaning far out to stab downward with Stormbringer. The
runesword sank cleanly into the demon's right eye and it
roared, letting go of Smiorgan, striking at the blade which
drew its energy from it, and as that energy passed into
the blade and thence to Elric, the albino grinned a frightful grin so that, for a second, Smiorgan became more
frightened of his friend than he had been of the demon.
The demon began to dematerialize, its only means of escape from the sword which drank its life-force, but more
of Saxif D'Aan's rogues were behind it, and their blades
rattled as they sought the pair.

Elric swung himself back over the rail, balanced pre-
cariously on the yard as he slashed at their attackers, yell-
ing the old battle-cries of his people. Smiorgan could do
little but watch. He noted that Saxif D'Aan was no longer
on deck and he shouted urgently to Elric:

"Elric! Saxif D'Aan. He seeks out the girl."

Elric now took the attack to the pirates, and they
were more than anxious to avoid the moaning runesword,
some even leaping into the sea rather than encounter it.
Swiftly the two leaped from yard to yard until they were
again upon the deck.

"What does he fear? Why does he not use more sorcery?" panted Count Smiorgan, as they ran toward the cabin.

"I have summoned the one who rides the horse," Elric told him. "I had so little time—and I could tell you nothing of it, knowing that Saxif D'Aan would read my intention in your mind, if he could not in mine!"

The cabin doors were firmly secured from the inside. Elric began to hack at them with the black sword.

But the door resisted as it should not have resisted. "Sealed by sorcery and I've no means of unsealing it," said the albino.

"Will he kill her?"

"I don't know. He might try to take her into some other plane. We must—"

Hooves clattered on the deck and the white stallion reared behind them, only now it had a rider, clad in bright purple and yellow armor. He was bareheaded and youthful, though there were several old scars upon his face. His hair was thick and curly and blond and his eyes were a deep blue.

He drew tightly upon his reins, steadying the horse. He looked piercingly at Elric. "Was it you, Melnibonéan, who opened the pathway for me?"

"It was."

"Then I thank you, though I cannot repay you."

"You have repaid me," Elric told him, then drew Smiorgan aside as the rider leaned forward and spurred his horse directly at the closed doors, smashing through as though they were rotted cotton.

There came a terrible cry from within and then Earl Saxif D'Aan, hampered by his complicated robes of gold, rushed from the cabin, seizing a sword from the hand of the nearest corpse, darting Elric a look not so much of hatred but of bewildered agony, as he turned to face the blond rider.

The rider had dismounted now and came from the cabin, one arm around the shivering girl, Vassliss, one hand upon the reins of his horse, and he said, sorrowfully:

"You did me a great wrong, Earl Saxif D'Aan, but you

did Gratyesha an infinitely more terrible one. Now you must pay."

Saxif D'Aan paused, drawing a deep breath, and when he looked up again, his eyes were steady, his dignity had returned.

"Must I pay in full?" he said.

"In full."

"It is all I deserve," said Saxif D'Aan. "I escaped my doom for many years, but I could not escape the knowledge of my crime. She loved me, you know. Not you."

"She loved us both, I think. But the love she gave you was her entire soul and I should not want that from any woman."

"You would be the loser, then."

"You never knew how much she loved you."

"Only—only afterward. . . ."

"I pity you, Earl Saxif D'Aan." The young man gave the reins of his horse to the girl, and he drew his sword. "We are strange rivals, are we not?"

"You have been all these years in Limbo, where I banished you—in that garden on Melniboné?"

"All these years. Only my horse could follow you. The horse of Tendric, my father, also of Melniboné, and also a sorcerer."

"If I had known that, then, I'd have slain you cleanly and sent the horse to Limbo."

"Jealousy weakened you, Earl Saxif D'Aan. But now we fight as we should have fought then—man to man, with steel, for the hand of the one who loves us both. It is more than you deserve."

"Much more," agreed the sorcerer. And he brought up his sword to lunge at the young man who, Smiorgan guessed, could only be Prince Carolak himself.

The fight was predetermined. Saxif D'Aan knew that, if Carolak did not. Saxif D'Aan's skill in arms was up to the standard of any Melnibonéan nobleman, but it could not match the skill of a professional soldier, who had fought for his life time after time.

Back and forth across the deck, while Saxif D'Aan's rascals looked on in openmouthed astonishment, the rivals fought a duel which should have been fought and resolved two centuries before, while the girl they both plainly thought was the reincarnation of Gratyesha watched them with as much concern as might her original have watched when Saxif D'Aan first encountered Prince Carolak in the gardens of his palace, so long ago.

Saxif D'Aan fought well, and Carolak fought nobly, for on many occasions he avoided an obvious advantage, but at length Saxif D'Aan threw away his sword, crying: "Enough. I'll give you your vengeance, Prince Carolak. I'll let you take the girl. But you'll not give me your damned mercy—you'll not take my pride."

And Carolak nodded, stepped forward, and struck straight for Saxif D'Aan's heart.

The blade entered clean and Earl Saxif D'Aan should have died, but he did not. He crawled along the deck until he reached the base of the mast, and he rested his back against it, while the blood pumped from the wounded heart. And he smiled.

"It appears," he said faintly, "that I cannot die, so long have I sustained my life by sorcery. I am no longer a man."

He did not seem pleased by this thought, but Prince Carolak, stepping forward and leaning over him, reassured him. "You will die," he promised, "soon."

"What will you do with her—with Gratyesha?"

"Her name is Vassliss," said Count Smiorgan insistently. "She is a merchant's daughter, from Jharkor."

"She must make up her own mind," Carolak said, ignoring Smiorgan.

Earl Saxif D'Aan turned glazed eyes on Elric. "I must thank you," he said. "You brought me the one who could bring me peace, though I feared him."

"Is that why, I wonder, your sorcery was so weak against me?" Elric said. "Because you wished Carolak to come and release you from your guilt?"

"Possibly, Elric. You are wiser in some matters, it seems, than am I."

"What of the Crimson Gate?" Smiorgan growled. "Can

THE SAILOR ON THE SEAS OF FATE 107

that be opened? Have you still the power, Earl Saxif
D'Aan?"

"I think so." From the folds of his bloodstained gar-
ments of gold, the sorcerer produced a large crystal which
shone with the deep colors of a ruby. "This will not only
lead you to the gate, it will enable you to pass through,
only I must warn you . . ." Saxif D'Aan began to cough.
"The ship—" he gasped, "the ship—like my body—has
been sustained by means of sorcery—therefore . . ." His
head slumped forward. He raised it with a huge effort
and stared beyond them at the girl who still held the reins
of the white stallion. "Farewell, Gratyesha, Princess of
Fwem-Omeyo. I loved you." The eyes remained fixed
upon her, but they were dead eyes now.

Carolak turned back to look at the girl. "How do you
call yourself, Gratyesha?"

"They call me Vassliss," she told him. She smiled up
into his youthful, battle-scarred face. "That is what they
call me, Prince Carolak."

"You know who I am?"

"I know you now."

"Will you come with me, Gratyesha? Will you be my
bride, at last, in the strange new lands I have found, beyond the world?"

"I will come," she said.

He helped her up into the saddle of his white stallion
and climbed so that he sat behind her. He bowed to Elric
of Melniboné. "I thank you again, Sir Sorcerer, though I
never thought to be helped by one of the royal blood of
Melniboné."

Elric's expression was not without humor. "In Melniboné," he said, "I'm told it's tainted blood."

"Tainted with mercy, perhaps."

"Perhaps."

Prince Carolak saluted them. "I hope you find peace,
Prince Elric, as I have found it."

"I fear my peace will more resemble that which Saxif
D'Aan found," Elric said grimly. "Nonetheless, I thank
you for your good words, Prince Carolak."

Then Carolak, laughing, had ridden his horse for the rail, leaped it, and vanished.

There was a silence upon the ship. The remaining ruffians looked uncertainly from one to the other. Elric addressed them:

"Know you this—I have the key to the Crimson Gate —and only I have the knowledge to use it. Help me sail the ship, and you'll have freedom from this world! What say you?"

"Give us our orders, Captain," said a toothless individual, and he cackled with mirth. "It's the best offer we've had in a hundred years or more!"

VII

It was Smiorgan who first saw the Crimson Gate. He held the great red gem in his hand and pointed ahead.

"There! There, Elric! Saxif D'Aan has not betrayed us!"

The sea had begun to heave with huge, turbulent waves, and with the mainsail still tangled upon the deck, it was all that the crew could do to control the ship, but the chance of escape from the world of the blue sun made them work with every ounce of energy and, slowly, the golden battle-barge neared the towering crimson pillars.

The pillars rose from the gray, roaring water, casting a peculiar light upon the crests of the waves. They appeared to have little substance, and yet stood firm against the battering of the tons of water lashing around them.

"Let us hope they are wider apart than they look," said Elric. "It would be a hard enough task steering through them in calm waters, let alone this kind of sea."

"I'd best take the wheel, I think," said Count Smiorgan, handing Elric the gem, and he strode back up the tilting deck, climbing to the covered wheelhouse and relieving the frightened man who stood there.

There was nothing Elric could do but watch as Smiorgan turned the huge vessel into the waves, riding the tops as best he could, but sometimes descending with a rush which made Elric's heart rise to his mouth. All around them, then, the cliffs of water threatened, but the ship was taking another wave before the main force of water could crash onto her decks. For all this, Elric was quickly soaked through and, though sense told him he would be best below, he clung to the rail, watching as Smiorgan steered the ship with uncanny sureness toward the Crimson Gate.

And then the deck was flooded with red light and Elric was half blinded. Gray water flew everywhere; there came a dreadful scraping sound, then a snapping as oars broke against the pillars. The ship shuddered and began to turn, sideways to the wind, but Smiorgan forced her around and suddenly the quality of the light changed subtly, though the sea remained as turbulent as ever and Elric knew, deep within him, that overhead, beyond the heavy clouds, a yellow sun was burning again.

But now there came a creaking and a crashing from within the bowels of the battle-barge. The smell of mold, which Elric had noted earlier, became stronger, almost overpowering.

Smiorgan came hurrying back, having handed over the wheel. His face was pale again. "She's breaking up, Elric," he called out, over the noise of the wind and the waves. He staggered as a huge wall of water struck the ship and snatched away several planks from the deck. "She's falling apart, man!"

"Saxif D'Aan tried to warn us of this!" Elric shouted back. "As he was kept alive by sorcery, so was his ship. She was old before he sailed her to that world. While there, the sorcery which sustained her remained strong—but on this plane it has no power at all. Look!" And he pulled at a piece of the rail, crumbling the rotten wood with his fingers. "We must find a length of timber which is still good."

At that moment a yard came crashing from the mast and struck the deck, bouncing, then rolling toward them.

Elric crawled up the sloping deck until he could grasp the spar and test it. "This one's still good. Use your belt or whatever else you can and tie yourself to it!"

The wind wailed through the disintegrating rigging of the ship; the sea smashed at the sides, driving great holes below the waterline.

The ruffians who had crewed her were in a state of complete panic, some trying to unship small boats which crumbled even as they swung them out, others lying flat against the rotted decks and praying to whatever gods they still worshiped.

Elric strapped himself to the broken yard as firmly as he could and Smiorgan followed his example. The next wave to hit the ship full on lifted them with it, cleanly over what remained of the rail and into the chilling, shouting waters of that terrible sea.

Elric kept his mouth tight shut against swallowing too much water and reflected on the irony of his situation. It seemed that, having escaped so much, he was to die a very ordinary death, by drowning.

It was not long before his senses left him and he gave himself up to the swirling and somehow friendly waters of the ocean.

He awoke, struggling.

There were hands upon him. He strove to fight them off, but he was too weak. Someone laughed, a rough, good-humored sound.

The water no longer roared and crashed around him. The wind no longer howled. Instead there was a gentler movement. He heard waves lapping against timber. He was aboard another ship.

He opened his eyes, blinking in warm, yellow sunlight. Red-cheeked Vilmirian sailors grinned down at him. "You're a lucky man—if man you be!" said one.

"My friend?" Elric sought for Smiorgan.

"He was in better shape than were you. He's down in Duke Avan's cabin now."

"Duke Avan?" Elric knew the name, but in his dazed

condition could remember nothing to help him place the man. "You saved us?"

"Aye. We found you both drifting, tied to a broken yard carved with the strangest designs I've ever seen. A Melnibonéan craft, was she?"

"Yes, but rather old."

They helped him to his feet. They had stripped him of his clothes and wrapped him in woolen blankets. The sun was already drying his hair. He was very weak. He said:

"My sword?"

"Duke Avan has it, below."

"Tell him to be careful of it."

"We're sure he will."

"This way," said another. "The duke awaits you."

Book THREE

SAILING TO THE PAST

I

Elric sat back in the comfortable, well-padded chair and accepted the wine-cup handed him by his host. While Smiorgan ate his fill of the hot food provided for them, Elric and Duke Avan appraised one another.

Duke Avan was a man of about forty, with a square, handsome face. He was dressed in a gilded silver breastplate, over which was arranged a white cloak. His britches, tucked into black knee-length boots, were of cream-colored doeskin. On a small sea-table at his elbow rested his helmet, crested with scarlet feathers.

"I am honored, sir, to have you as my guest," said Duke Avan. "I know you to be Elric of Melniboné. I have been seeking you for several months, ever since news came to me that you had left your homeland (and your power) behind and were wandering, as it were, incognito in the Young Kingdoms."

"You know much, sir."

"I, too, am a traveler by choice. I almost caught up with you in Pikarayd, but I gather there was some sort of trouble there. You left quickly and then I lost your trail altogether. I was about to give up looking for your aid when, by the greatest of good fortune, I found you floating in the water!" Duke Avan laughed.

"You have the advantage of me," said Elric, smiling. "You raise many questions."

"He's Avan Astran of Old Hrolmar," grunted Count Smiorgan from the other side of a huge ham bone. "He's well known as an adventurer—explorer—trader. His reputation's the best. We can trust him, Elric."

"I recall the name now," Elric told the duke. "But why should you seek my aid?"

The smell of the food from the table had at last impinged and Elric got up. "Would you mind if I ate something while you explained, Duke Avan?"

115

"Eat your fill, Prince Elric. I am honored to have you as a guest."

"You have saved my life, sir. I have never had it saved so courteously!"

Duke Avan smiled. "I have never before had the pleasure of, let us say, catching so courteous a fish. If I were a superstitious man, Prince Elric, I should guess that some other force threw us together in this way."

"I prefer to think of it as coincidence," said the albino, beginning to eat. "Now, sir, tell me how I can aid you."

"I shall not hold you to any bargain, merely because I have been lucky enough to save your life," said Duke Avan Astran; "please bear that in mind."

"I shall, sir."

Duke Avan stroked the feathers of his helmet. "I have explored most of the world, as Count Smiorgan rightly says. I have been to your own Melniboné and I have even ventured east, to Elwher and the Unknown Kingdoms. I have been to Myyrrhn, where the Winged Folk live. I have traveled as far as World's Edge and hope one day to go beyond. But I have never crossed the Boiling Sea and I know only a small stretch of coast along the western continent—the continent that has no name. Have you been there, Elric, in your travels?"

The albino shook his head. "I seek experience of other cultures, other civilizations—that is why I travel. There has been nothing, so far, to take me there. The continent is largely uninhabited, and then, where it is inhabited, only by savages, is it not?"

"So we are told."

"You have other intelligence?"

"You know that there is some evidence," said Duke Avan in a deliberate tone, "that your own ancestors came originally from that mainland?"

"Evidence?" Elric pretended lack of interest. "A few legends, that is all."

"One of those legends speaks of a city older than dreaming Imrryr. A city that still exists in the deep jungles of the west."

Elric recalled his conversation with Earl Saxif D'Aan, and he smiled to himself. "You mean R'lin K'ren A'a?"

"Aye. A strange name." Duke Avan Astran leaned forward, his eyes alight with delighted curiosity. "You pronounce it more fluently than could I. You speak the secret tongue, the High Tongue, the Speech of Kings. . . ."

"Of course."

"You are forbidden to teach it to any but your own children, are you not?"

"You appear conversant with the customs of Melniboné, Duke Avan," Elric said, his lids falling so that they half covered his eyes. He leaned back in his seat as he bit into a piece of fresh bread with relish. "Do you know what the words mean?"

"I have been told that they mean simply 'Where the High Ones Meet' in the ancient speech of Melniboné," Duke Avan Astran told him.

Elric inclined his head. "That is so. Doubtless only a small town, in reality. Where local chiefs gathered, perhaps once a year, to discuss the price of grain."

"You believe that, Prince Elric?"

Elric inspected a covered dish. He helped himself to veal in a rich, sweet sauce. "No," he said.

"You believe, then, that there was an ancient civilization even before your own, from which your own culture sprang? You believe that R'lin K'ren A'a is still there, somewhere in the jungles of the west?"

Elric waited until he had swallowed. He shook his head.

"No," he said. "I believe that it does not exist at all."

"You are not curious about your ancestors?"

"Should I be?"

"They were said to be different in character from those who founded Melniboné. Gentler. . . ." Duke Avan Astran looked deep into Elric's face.

Elric laughed. "You are an intelligent man, Duke Avan of Old Hrolmar. You are a perceptive man. Oh, and indeed you are a cunning man, sir!"

Duke Avan grinned at the compliment. "And you know

much more of the legends than you are admitting, if I
am not mistaken."

"Possibly." Elric sighed as the food warmed him. "We
are known as a secretive people, we of Melniboné."

"Yet," said Duke Avan, "you seem untypical. Who else
would desert an empire to travel in lands where his very
race was hated?"

"An emperor rules better, Duke Avan Astran, if he has
close knowledge of the world in which he rules."

"Melniboné rules the Young Kingdoms no longer."

"Her power is still great. But that, anyway, was not
what I meant. I am of the opinion that the Young Kingdoms offer something which Melniboné has lost."

"Vitality?"

"Perhaps."

"Humanity!" grunted Count Smiorgan Baldhead. "That
is what your race has lost, Prince Elric. I say nothing of
you—but look at Earl Saxif D'Aan. How can one so wise
be such a simpleton? He lost everything—pride, love,
power—because he had no humanity. And what humanity
he had—why, it destroyed him."

"Some say it will destroy me," said Elric, "but perhaps
'humanity' is, indeed, what I seek to bring to Melniboné, Count Smiorgan."

"Then you will destroy your kingdom!" said Smiorgan
bluntly. "It is too late to save Melniboné."

"Perhaps I can help you find what you seek, Prince
Elric," said Duke Avan Astran quietly. "Perhaps there is
time to save Melniboné, if you feel such a mighty nation
is in danger."

"From within," said Elric. "But I speak too freely."

"For a Melnibonéan, that is true."

"How did you come to hear of this city?" Elric wished
to know. "No other man I have met in the Young Kingdoms has heard of R'lin K'ren A'a."

"It is marked on a map I have."

Deliberately, Elric chewed his meat and swallowed it.
"The map is doubtless a forgery."

"Perhaps. Do you recall anything else of the legend of
R'lin K'ren A'a?"

"There is the story of the Creature Doomed to Live." Elric pushed the food aside and poured wine for himself. "The city is said to have received its name because the Lords of the Higher Worlds once met there to decide the rules of the Cosmic Struggle. They were overheard by the one inhabitant of the city who had not flown when they came. When they discovered him, they doomed him to remain alive forever, carrying the frightful knowledge in his head. . . ."

"I have heard that story, too. But the one that interests me is that the inhabitants of R'lin K'ren A'a never returned to their city. Instead they struck northward and crossed the sea. Some reached an island we now call Sorcerer's Isle while others went farther—blown by a great storm—and came at length to a larger island inhabited by dragons whose venom caused all it touched to burn . . . to Melniboné, in fact."

"And you wish to test the truth of that story. Your interest is that of a scholar?"

Duke Avan laughed. "Partly. But my main interest in R'lin K'ren A'a is more materialistic. For your ancestors left a great treasure behind them when they fled their city. Particularly they abandoned an image of Arioch, the Lord of Chaos—a monstrous image, carved in jade, whose eyes were two huge, identical gems of a kind unknown anywhere else in all the lands of the Earth. Jewels from another plane of existence. Jewels which could reveal all the secrets of the Higher Worlds, of the past and the future, of the myriad planes of the cosmos. . . ."

"All cultures have similar legends. Wishful thinking, Duke Avan, that is all. . . ."

"But the Melnibonéans had a culture unlike any others. The Melnibonéans are not true men, as you well know. Their powers are superior, their knowledge far greater. . . ."

"It was once thus," Elric said. "But that great power and knowledge is not mine. I have only a fragment of it. . . ."

"I did not seek you in Bakshaan and later in Jadmar because I believed you could verify what I have heard. I did not cross the sea to Filkhar, then to Argimiliar and at

last to Pikarayd because I thought you would instantly
confirm all that I have spoken of—I sought you because
I think you the only man who would wish to accompany
me on a voyage which would give us the truth or false-
hood to these legends once and for all."

Elric tilted his head and drained his wine-cup.

"Cannot you do that for yourself? Why should you
desire my company on the expedition? From what I have
heard of you, Duke Avan, you are not one who needs
support in his venturings. . . ."

Duke Avan laughed. "I went alone to Elwher when my
men deserted me in the Weeping Waste. It is not in my
nature to know physical fear. But I have survived my
travels this long because I have shown proper foresight
and caution before setting off. Now it seems I must face
dangers I cannot anticipate—sorcery, perhaps. It struck
me, therefore, that I needed an ally who had some experience of fighting sorcery. And since I would have no
truck with the ordinary kind of wizard such as Pan Tang
spawns, you were my only choice. You seek knowledge,
Prince Elric, just as I do. Indeed, it could be said that if it
had not been for your yearning for knowledge, your cousin would never have attempted to usurp the Ruby Throne
of Melniboné. . . ."

"Enough of that," Elric said bitterly. "Let's talk of
this expedition. Where is the map?"

"You will accompany me?"

"Show me the map."

Duke Avan drew a scroll from his pouch. "Here it is."

"Where did you find it?"

"On Melniboné."

"You have been there recently?" Elric felt anger rise
in him.

Duke Avan raised a hand. "I went there with a group
of traders and I gave much for a particular casket which
had been sealed, it seemed, for an eternity. Within that
casket was this map." He spread out the scroll on the
table. Elric recognized the style and the script—the old
High Speech of Melniboné. It was a map of part of the
western continent—more than he had ever seen on any

other map. It showed a great river winding into the interior for a hundred miles or more. The river appeared to flow through a jungle and then divide into two rivers which later rejoined. The "island" of land thus formed had a black circle marked on it. Against this circle, in the involved writing of ancient Melniboné, was the name R'lin K'ren A'a. Elric inspected the scroll carefully. It did not seem to be a forgery.

"Is this all you found?" he asked.

"The scroll was sealed and this was embedded in the seal," Duke Avan said, handing something to Elric.

Elric held the object in his palm. It was a tiny ruby of a red so deep as to seem black at first, but when he turned it into the light he saw an image at the center of the ruby and he recognized that image. He frowned, then he said, "I will agree to your proposal, Duke Avan. Will you let me keep this?"

"Do you know what it is?"

"No. But I should like to find out. There is a memory somewhere in my head. . . ."

"Very well, take it. I will keep the map."

"When did you have it in mind to set off?"

Duke Avan's smile was sardonic. "We are already sailing around the southern coast to the Boiling Sea."

"There are few who have returned from that ocean," Elric murmured bitterly. He glanced across the table and saw that Smiorgan was imploring with his eyes for Elric not to have any part of Duke Avan's scheme. Elric smiled at his friend. "The adventure is to my taste."

Miserably, Smiorgan shrugged. "It seems it will be a little longer before I return to the Purple Towns."

The coast of Lormyr had disappeared in warm mist and Duke Avan Astran's schooner dipped its graceful prow toward the west and the Boiling Sea.

The Vilmirian crew of the schooner were used to a less demanding climate and more casual work than this and they went about their tasks, it seemed to Elric, with something of an aggrieved air.

Standing beside Elric in the ship's poop, Count Smiorgan Baldhead wiped sweat from his pate and growled: "Vilmirians are a lazy lot, Prince Elric. Duke Avan needs real sailors for a voyage of this kind. I could have picked him a crew, given the chance. . . ."

Elric smiled. "Neither of us was given the chance, Count Smiorgan. It was a fait accompli. He's a clever man, Duke Astran."

"It is not a cleverness I entirely respect, for he offered us no real choice. A free man is a better companion than a slave, says the old aphorism."

"Why did you not disembark when you had the chance, then, Count Smiorgan?"

"Because of the promise of treasure," said the black-bearded man frankly. "I would return with honor to the Purple Towns. Forget you not that I commanded the fleet that was lost. . . ."

Elric understood.

"My motives are straightforward," said Smiorgan. "Yours are much more complicated. You seem to desire danger as other men desire lovemaking or drinking—as if in danger you find forgetfulness."

"Is that not true of many professional soldiers?"

"You are not a mere professional soldier, Elric. That you know as well as I."

"Yet few of the dangers I have faced have helped me forget," Elric pointed out. "Rather they have strengthened the reminder of what I am—of the dilemma I face. My own instincts war against the traditions of my race." Elric drew a deep, melancholy breath. "I go where danger is because I think that an answer might lie there—some reason for all this tragedy and paradox. Yet I know I shall never find it."

"But it is why you sail to R'lin K'ren A'a, eh? You hope that your remote ancestors had the answer you need?"

"R'lin K'ren A'a is a myth. Even should the map prove genuine what shall we find but a few ruins? Imrryr has stood for ten thousand years and she was built at least two centuries after my people settled on Melniboné. Time will have taken R'lin K'ren A'a away."

"And this statue, this Jade Man, Avan spoke of?"

"If the statue ever existed, it could have been looted at any time in the past hundred centuries."

"And the Creature Doomed to Live?"

"A myth."

"But you hope, do you not, that it is all as Duke Avan says . . . ?" Count Smiorgan put a hand on Elric's arm. "Do you not?"

Elric stared ahead, into the writhing steam which rose from the sea. He shook his head.

"No, Count Smiorgan. I *fear* that it is all as Duke Avan says."

The wind blew whimsically and the schooner's passage was slow as the heat grew greater and the crew sweated still more and murmured fearfully. And upon each face, now, was a stricken look.

Only Duke Avan seemed to retain his confidence. He called to them all to take heart; he told them that they should all be rich soon; and he gave orders for the oars to be unshipped, for the wind could no longer be trusted. They grumbled at this, stripping off their shirts to reveal skins as red as cooked lobsters. Duke Avan made a joke of that. But the Vilmirians no longer laughed at his jokes as they had done in the milder seas of their home waters.

Around the ship the sea bubbled and roared, and they navigated by their few instruments, for the steam obscured everything.

Once a green thing erupted from the sea and glared at them before disappearing.

They ate and slept little and Elric rarely left the poop. Count Smiorgan bore the heat silently and Duke Avan, seemingly oblivious to any discomfort, went cheerfully about the ship, calling encouragement to his men.

Count Smiorgan was fascinated by the waters. He had

heard of them, but never crossed them. "These are only the outer reaches of this sea, Elric," he said in some wonder. "Think what it must be like at the middle."

Elric grinned. "I would rather not. As it is, I fear I'll be boiled to death before another day has passed."

Passing by, Duke Avan heard him and clapped him on the shoulder. "Nonsense, Prince Elric! The steam is good for you! There is nothing healthier!" Seemingly with pleasure, Duke Avan stretched his limbs. "It cleans all the poisons from the system."

Count Smiorgan offered him a glowering look and Duke Avan laughed. "Be of better cheer, Count Smiorgan. According to my charts—such as they are—a couple of days will see us nearing the coasts of the western continent."

"The thought fails to raise my spirits very greatly," said Count Smiorgan, but he smiled, infected by Avan's good humor.

But shortly thereafter the sea grew slowly less frenetic and the steam began to disperse until the heat became more tolerable.

At last they emerged into a calm ocean beneath a shimmering blue sky in which hung a red-gold sun.

But three of the Vilmirian crew had died to cross the Boiling Sea, and four more had a sickness in them which made them cough a great deal, and shiver, and cry out in the night.

For a while they were becalmed, but at last a soft wind began to blow and fill the schooner's sails and soon they had sighted their first land—a little yellow island where they found fruit and a spring of fresh water. Here, too, they buried the three men who had succumbed to the sickness of the Boiling Sea, for the Vilmirians had refused to have them buried in the ocean on the grounds that the bodies would be "stewed like meat in a pot."

While the schooner lay at anchor, just off the island, Duke Avan called Elric to his cabin and showed him, for a second time, that ancient map.

Pale golden sunlight filtered through the cabin's ports

and fell upon the old parchment, beaten from the skin of a beast long since extinct, as Elric and Duke Avan Astran of Old Hrolmar bent over it.

"See," Duke Avan said, pointing. "This island's marked. The map's scale seems reasonably accurate. Another three days and we shall be at the mouth of the river."

Elric nodded. "But it would be wise to rest here for a while until our strength is fully restored and the morale of the crew is raised higher. There are reasons, after all, why men have avoided the jungles of the west over the centuries."

"Certainly there are savages there—some say they are not even human—but I'm confident we can deal with those dangers. I have much experience of strange territories, Prince Elric."

"But you said yourself you feared other dangers."

"True. Very well, we'll do as you suggest."

On the fourth day a strong wind began to blow from the east and they raised anchor. The schooner leaped over the waves under only half her canvas and the crew saw this as a good omen.

"They are mindless fools," Smiorgan said as they stood clinging to the rigging in the prow. "The time will come when they will wish they were suffering the cleaner hardships of the Boiling Sea. This journey, Elric, could benefit none of us, even if the riches of R'lin K'ren A'a are still there."

But Elric did not answer. He was lost in strange thoughts, unusual thoughts for him, for he was remembering his childhood, his mother and his father. They had been the last true rulers of the Bright Empire—proud, insouciant, cruel. They had expected him—perhaps because of his strange albinism—to restore the glories of Melniboné. Instead he threatened to destroy what was left of that glory. They, like himself, had had no real place in this new age of the Young Kingdoms, but they had refused to acknowledge it. This journey to the western continent, to the land of his ancestors, had a peculiar attraction for him. Here no new nations had emerged. The continent had, as far as he knew, remained the same since R'lin K'ren A'a had been abandoned. The jungles would be the jungles his folk had known, the land would be the land that had given birth to his peculiar race, molded the character of its people with their somber pleasures, their melancholy arts, and their dark delights. Had his ancestors felt this agony of knowledge, this impotence in the face of the understanding that existence had no point, no purpose, no hope? Was this why they had built their civilization in that particular pattern, why they had disdained the more placid, spiritual values of mankind's philosophers? He knew that many of the intellectuals of the Young Kingdoms pitied the powerful folk of Melniboné as mad. But if they had been mad and if they had imposed a madness upon the world that had lasted a hundred centuries, what had made them so? Perhaps the secret did lie in R'lin K'ren A'a—not in any tangible form, but in the ambience created by the dark jungles and the deep, old rivers. Perhaps here, at last, he would be able to feel at one with himself.

He ran his fingers through his milk-white hair and there was a kind of innocent anguish in his crimson eyes. He might be the last of his kind and yet he was unlike his kind. Smiorgan had been wrong. Elric knew that everything that existed had its opposite. In danger he might find peace. And yet, of course, in peace there was danger. Being an imperfect creature in an imperfect world he would always know paradox. And that was why in paradox there was always a kind of truth. That was why philosophers and soothsayers flourished. In a perfect world there would be no place for them. In an imperfect world the mysteries were always without solution and that was why there was always a great choice of solutions.

It was on the morning of the third day that the coast was sighted and the schooner steered her way through the sandbanks of the great delta and anchored, at last, at the mouth of the dark and nameless river.

III

Evening came and the sun began to set over the black outlines of the massive trees. A rich, ancient smell came from the jungle and through the twilight echoed the cries of strange birds and beasts. Elric was impatient to begin the quest up the river. Sleep—never welcome—was now impossible to achieve. He stood unmoving on the deck, his eyes hardly blinking, his brain barely active, as if expecting something to happen to him. The rays of the sun stained his face and threw black shadows over the deck and then it was dark and still under the moon and the stars. He wanted the jungle to absorb him. He wanted to be one with the trees and the shrubs and the creeping beasts. He wanted thought to disappear. He drew the heavily scented air into his lungs as if that alone would make him become what at that moment he desired to be. The drone of insects became a murmuring voice that called him into the heart of the old, old forest. And yet he could not move—could not answer. And at length Count Smiorgan came up on deck and touched his shoulder and said something and passively he went below to his bunk and wrapped himself in his cloak and lay there, still listening to the voice of the jungle.

Even Duke Avan seemed in a more introspective mood than usual when they upped anchor the next morning and began to row against the sluggish current. There were few gaps in the foliage above their heads and they had the impression that they were entering a huge, gloomy tunnel, leaving the sunlight behind with the sea. Bright plants twined among the vines that hung from the leafy canopy and caught in the ship's masts as they moved. Ratlike animals with long arms swung through the branches and peered at them with bright, knowing eyes. The river turned and the sea was no longer in sight. Shafts of sunlight filtered down to the deck and the light had a greenish tinge to it. Elric became more alert than he had ever been since he agreed to accompany Duke Avan. He took a keen interest in every detail of the jungle and the black river over which moved schools of insects like agitated clouds of mist and in which blossoms drifted like drops of blood in ink. Everywhere were rustlings, sudden squawks, barks and wet noises made by fish or river animals as they hunted the prey disturbed by the ship's oars which cut into the great clumps of weed and sent the things that hid there scurrying. The others began to complain of insect bites, but Elric was not troubled by them, perhaps because no insect could desire his deficient blood.

Duke Avan passed him on the deck. The Vilmirian slapped at his forehead. "You seem more cheerful, Prince Elric."

Elric smiled absently. "Perhaps I am."

"I must admit I personally find all this a bit oppressive. I'll be glad when we reach the city."

"You are still convinced you'll find it?"

"I'll be convinced otherwise when I've explored every inch of the island we're bound for."

So absorbed had he become in the atmosphere of the jungle that Elric was hardly aware of the ship or his companions. The ship beat very slowly up the river, moving at little more than walking speed.

A few days passed, but Elric scarcely noticed, for the jungle did not change—and then the river widened and the canopy parted and the wide, hot sky was suddenly full of huge birds crowding upward as the ship disturbed them. All but Elric were pleased to be under the open sky again and spirits rose. Elric went below.

The attack on the ship came almost immediately. There was a whistling noise and a scream and a sailor writhed and fell over clutching at a gray thin semicircle of something which had buried itself in his stomach. An upper yard came crashing to the deck, bringing sail and rigging with it. A headless body took four paces toward the poop deck before collapsing, the blood pumping from the obscene hole that was its neck. And everywhere was the thin whistling noise. Elric heard the sounds from below and came back instantly, buckling on his sword. The first face he saw was Smiorgan's. The bald-pated man looked perturbed as he crouched against a rail on the starboard side. Elric had the impression of gray blurs whistling past, slashing into flesh and rigging, wood and canvas. Some fell to the deck and he saw that they were thin disks of crystalline rock, about a foot in diameter. They were being hurled from both banks of the river and there was no protection against them.

He tried to see who was throwing the disks and glimpsed something moving in the trees along the right bank. Then the disks ceased suddenly and there was a pause before some of the sailors dashed across the deck to seek better cover. Duke Avan suddenly appeared in the stern. He had unsheathed his sword.

"Get below. Get your bucklers and any armor you can find. Bring bows. Arm yourselves, men, or you're finished."

And as he spoke their attackers broke from the trees and began to wade into the water. No more disks came and it seemed likely they had exhausted their supply.

"By Chardros!" Avan gasped. "Are these real creatures or some sorcerer's conjurings?"

The things were essentially reptilian but with feathery crests and neck wattles, though their faces were almost human. Their forelegs were like the arms and hands of men, but their hindlegs were incredibly long and storklike. Balanced on these legs, their bodies towered over the water. They carried great clubs in which slits had been cut and doubtless these were what they used to hurl the crystalline disks. Staring at their faces, Elric was horrified. In some subtle way they reminded him of the characteristic faces of his own folk—the folk of Melniboné. Were these creatures his cousins? Or were they a species from which his people had evolved? He stopped asking the questions as an intense hatred for the creatures filled him. They were obscene: sight of them brought bile into his throat. Without thinking, he drew Stormbringer from its sheath.

The Black Sword began to howl and the familiar black radiance spilled from it. The runes carved into its blade pulsed a vivid scarlet which turned slowly to a deep purple and then to black once more.

The creatures were wading through the water on their stiltlike legs and they paused when they saw the sword, glancing at one another. And they were not the only ones unnerved by the sight, for Duke Avan and his men paled, too.

"Gods!" Avan yelled. "I know not which I prefer the look of—those who attack us or that which defends us!"

"Stay well away from that sword," Smiorgan warned. "It has the habit of killing more than its master chooses."

And now the reptilian savages were upon them, clutching at the ship's rails as the armed sailors rushed back on deck to meet the attack.

Clubs came at Elric from all sides, but Stormbringer shrieked and parried each blow. He held the sword in both hands, whirling it this way and that, plowing great gashes in the scaly bodies.

The creatures hissed and opened red mouths in agony and rage while their thick, black blood sank into the waters of the river. Although from the legs upward they were only slightly larger than a tall, well-built man, they had more vitality than any human and the deepest cuts hardly seemed to affect them, even when administered by Stormbringer. Elric was astonished at this resistance to the sword's power. Often a nick was enough for the sword to draw a man's soul from him. These things seemed immune. Perhaps they had no souls. . . .

He fought on, his hatred giving him strength.

But elsewhere on the ship the sailors were being routed. Rails were torn off and the great clubs crushed planks and brought down more rigging. The savages were intent on destroying the ship as well as the crew. And there was little doubt, now, that they would be successful.

Avan shouted to Elric. "By the names of all the gods, Prince Elric, can you not summon some further sorcery? We are doomed else!"

Elric knew Avan spoke truth. All around him the ship

was being gradually pulled apart by the hissing reptilian
creatures. Most of them had sustained horrible wounds
from the defenders, but only one or two had collapsed.
Elric began to suspect that they did, in fact, fight supernatural enemies.

He backed away and sought shelter beneath a half-
crushed doorway as he tried to concentrate on a method
of calling upon supernatural aid.

He was panting with exhaustion and he clung to a
beam as the ship rocked back and forth in the water. He
fought to clear his head.

And then the incantation came to him. He was not sure
if it was appropriate, but it was the only one he could
recall. His ancestors had made pacts, thousands of years
before, with all the elementals who controlled the animal
world. In the past he had summoned help from various
of these spirits but never from the one he now sought to
call. From his mouth began to issue the ancient, beautiful, and convoluted words of Melniboné's High Speech.

"King with Wings! Lord of all that work and are not
seen, upon whose labors all else depends! Nnuuurrrr'c'c
of the Insect Folk, I summon thee!"

Save for the motion of the ship, Elric ceased to be aware
of all else happening around him. The sounds of the fight
dimmed and were heard no more as he sent his voice
out beyond his plane of the Earth into another—the
plane dominated by King Nnuuurrrr'c'c of the Insects,
paramount lord of his people.

In his ears now Elric heard a buzzing and gradually the
buzzing formed itself in words.

"Who art thou, mortal? What right hast thee to summon me?"

"I am Elric, ruler of Melniboné. My ancestors aided
thee, Nnuuurrrr'c'c."

"Aye—but long ago."

"And it is long ago that they last called on thee for thine
aid!"

"True. What aid dost thou now require, Elric of Melniboné?"

"Look upon my plane. Thou wilt see that I am in danger. Canst thou abolish this danger, friend of the Insects?"

Now a filmy shape formed and could be seen as if through several layers of cloudy silk. Elric tried to keep his eyes upon it, but it kept leaving his field of vision and then returning for a few moments. He knew that he looked into another plane of the Earth.

"Canst thou help me, Nnuuurrrr'c'c?"

"Hast thou no patron of thine own species? Some Lord of Chaos who can aid thee?"

"My patron is Arioch and he is a temperamental demon at best. These days he aids me little."

"Then I must send thee allies, mortal. But call upon me no more when this is done."

"I shall not summon thee again, Nnuuurrrr'c'c."

The layers of film disappeared and with them the shape.

The noise of the battle crashed once again on Elric's consciousness and he heard with sharper clarity than before the screams of the sailors and the hissing of the reptilian savages and when he looked out from his shelter he saw that at least half the crew were dead.

As he came on deck Smiorgan ran up. "I thought you slain, Elric! What became of you?" He was plainly relieved to see his friend still lived.

"I sought aid from another plane—but it does not seem to have materialized."

"I'm thinking we're doomed and had best try to swim downstream away from here and seek a hiding place in the jungle," Smiorgan said.

"What of Duke Avan? Is he dead?"

"He lives. But those creatures are all but impervious to our weapons. This ship will sink ere long." Smiorgan lurched as the deck tilted and he reached out to grab a trailing rope, letting his long sword dangle by its wristthong. "They are not attacking the stern at present. We can slip into the water there. . . ."

"I made a bargain with Duke Avan," Elric reminded the islander. "I cannot desert him."

"Then we'll all perish!"

"What's that?" Elric bent his head, listening intently.

"I hear nothing."

It was a whine which deepened in tone until it became a drone. Now Smiorgan heard it also and looked about him, seeking the source of the sound. And suddenly he gasped, pointing upward. "Is that the aid you sought?"

There was a vast cloud of them, black against the blue of the sky. Every so often the sun would flash on a dazzling color—a rich blue, green, or red. They came spiraling down toward the ship and now both sides fell silent, staring skyward.

The flying things were like huge dragonflies and the brightness and richness of their coloring was breathtaking. It was their wings which made the droning sound which now began to increase in loudness and heighten in pitch as the huge insects sped nearer.

Realizing that they were the object of the attack the reptile men stumbled backward on their long legs, trying to reach the shore before the gigantic insects were upon them.

But it was too late for flight.

The dragonflies settled on the savages until nothing could be seen of their bodies. The hissing increased and sounded almost pitiful as the insects bore their victims down to the surface and then inflicted on them whatever terrible death it was. Perhaps they stung with their tails—it was not possible for the watchers to see.

Sometimes a storklike leg would emerge from the water and thrash in the air for a moment. But soon, just as the reptiles were covered by the insect bodies, so were their cries drowned by the strange and blood-chilling humming that arose on all sides.

A sweating Duke Avan, sword still in hand, ran up the deck. "Is this your doing, Prince Elric?"

Elric looked on with satisfaction, but the others were plainly disgusted. "It was," he said.

"Then I thank you for your aid. This ship is holed in a dozen places and is letting in water at a terrible rate. It's a wonder we have not yet sunk. I've given orders to begin rowing and I hope we make it to the island in time." He pointed upstream. "There, you can just see it."

"What if there are more of those savages there?" Smiorgan asked.

Avan smiled grimly, indicating the farther shore. "Look." On their peculiar legs a dozen or more of the reptiles were fleeing into the jungle, having witnessed the fate of their comrades. "They'll be reluctant to attack us again, I think."

Now the huge dragonflies were rising into the air again and Avan turned away as he glimpsed what they had left behind. "By the gods, you work fierce sorcery, Prince Elric! Ugh!"

Elric smiled and shrugged. "It is effective, Duke Avan." He sheathed his runesword. It seemed reluctant to enter the scabbard and it moaned as if in resentment.

Smiorgan glanced at it. "That blade looks as if it will want to feast soon, Elric, whether you desire it or not."

"Doubtless it will find something to feed on in the forest," said the albino. He stepped over a piece of broken mast and went below.

Count Smiorgan Baldhead looked at the new scum on the surface of the water and he shuddered.

IV

The wrecked schooner was almost awash when the crew clambered overboard with lines and began the task of dragging it up the mud that formed the banks of the island. Before them was a wall of foliage that seemed impenetrable. Smiorgan followed Elric, lowering himself into the shallows. They began to wade ashore.

As they left the water and set foot on the hard, baked earth, Smiorgan stared at the forest. No wind moved the trees and a peculiar silence had descended. No birds called from the trees, no insects buzzed, there were none of the barks and cries of animals they had heard on their journey upriver.

"Those supernatural friends of yours seem to have

frightened more than the savages away," the black-bearded man murmured. "This place seems lifeless."

Elric nodded. "It is strange."

Duke Avan joined them. He had discarded his finery—ruined in the fight, anyway—and now wore a padded leather jerkin and doeskin breeches. His sword was at his side. "We'll have to leave most of our men behind with the ship," he said regretfully. "They'll make what repairs they can while we press on to find R'lin K'ren A'a." He tugged his light cloak about him. "Is it my imagination, or is there an odd atmosphere?"

"We have already remarked on it," Smiorgan said. "Life seems to have fled the island."

Duke Avan grinned. "If all we face is as timid, we have nothing further to fear. I must admit, Prince Elric, that had I wished you harm and then seen you conjure those monsters from thin air, I'd think twice about getting too close to you! Thank you, by the way, for what you did. We should have perished by now if it had not been for you."

"It was for my aid that you asked me to accompany you," Elric said wearily. "Let's eat and rest and then continue with our expedition."

A shadow passed over Duke Avan's face then. Something in Elric's manner had disturbed him.

Entering the jungle was no easy matter. Armed with axes the six members of the crew (all that could be spared) began to hack at the undergrowth. And still the unnatural silence prevailed. . . .

By nightfall they were less than half a mile into the forest and completely exhausted. The forest was so thick that there was barely room to pitch their tent. The only light in the camp came from the small, sputtering fire outside the tent. The crewmen slept where they could in the open.

Elric could not sleep, but now it was not the jungle which kept him awake. He was puzzled by the silence, for he was sure that it was not their presence which had driven all life away. There was not a single small rodent, bird, or insect anywhere to be seen. There were no traces of animal life. The island had been deserted of all but vegetation for a long while—perhaps for centuries or tens of centuries. He remembered another part of the old legend of R'lin K'ren A'a. It had been said that when the gods came to meet there not only the citizens fled, but also all the wildlife. Nothing had dared see the High Lords or listen to their conversation. Elric shivered, turning his white head this way and that on the rolled cloak that supported it, his crimson eyes tortured. If there were dangers on this island, they would be subtler dangers than those they had faced on the river.

The noise of their passage through the forest was the only sound to be heard on the island as they forced their way on the next morning.

With lodestone in one hand and map in the other, Duke Avan Astran sought to guide them, directing his men where to cut their path. But the going became even slower and it was obvious that no creatures had come this way for many ages.

By the fourth day they had reached a natural clearing of flat volcanic rock and found a spring there. Gratefully they made camp. Elric began to wash his face in the cool water when he heard a yell behind him. He sprang up. One of the crewmen was reaching for an arrow and fitting it to his bow.

"What is it?" Duke Avan called.

"I saw something, my lord!"

"Nonsense, there are no—"

"Look!" The man drew back the string and let fly into the upper terraces of the forest. Something did seem to stir then and Elric thought he saw a flash of gray among the trees.

"Did you see what kind of creature it was?" Smiorgan asked the man.

"No, master. I feared at first it was those reptiles again."

"They're too frightened to follow us onto this island," Duke Avan reassured him.

"I hope you're right," Smiorgan said nervously.

"Then what could it have been?" Elric wondered.

"I—I thought it was a man, master," the crewman stuttered.

Elric stared thoughtfully into the trees. "A man?"

Smiorgan asked, "You were hoping for this, Elric?"

"I am not sure. . . ."

Duke Avan shrugged. "More likely the shadow of a cloud passing over the trees. According to my calculations we should have reached the city by now."

"You think, after all, that it does not exist?" Elric said.

"I am beginning not to care, Prince Elric." The duke leaned against the bole of a huge tree, brushing aside a vine which touched his face. "Still there's naught else to do. The ship won't be ready to sail yet." He looked up into the branches. "I did not think I should miss those damned insects that plagued us on our way here. . . ."

The crewman who had shot the arrow suddenly shouted again. "There! I saw him! It is a man!"

While the others stared but failed to discern anything Duke Avan continued to lean against the tree. "You saw nothing. There is nothing here to see."

Elric turned toward him. "Give me the map and the lodestone, Duke Avan. I have a feeling I can find the way."

The Vilmirian shrugged, an expression of doubt on his square, handsome face. He handed the things over to Elric.

They rested the night and in the morning they continued, with Elric leading the way.

And at noon they broke out of the forest and saw the ruins of R'lin K'ren A'a.

V

Nothing grew among the ruins of the city. The streets were broken and the walls of the houses had fallen, but there were no weeds flowering in the cracks and it seemed that the city had but recently been brought down by an earthquake. Only one thing still stood intact, towering over the ruins. It was a gigantic statue of white, gray, and green jade—the statue of a naked youth with a face of almost feminine beauty that turned sightless eyes toward the north.

"The eyes!" Duke Avan Astran said. "They're gone!"

The others said nothing as they stared at the statue and the ruins surrounding it. The area was relatively small and the buildings had had little decoration. The inhabitants seemed to have been a simple, well-to-do folk—totally unlike the Melnibonéans of the Bright Empire. Elric could not believe that the people of R'lin K'ren A'a had been his ancestors. They had been too sane.

"The statue's already been looted," Duke Avan continued. "Our damned journey's been in vain!"

Elric laughed. "Did you really think you would be able to prise the Jade Man's eyes from their sockets, my lord?"

The statue was as tall as any tower of the Dreaming City and the head alone must have been the size of a reasonably large building. Duke Avan pursed his lips and refused to listen to Elric's mocking voice. "We may yet find the journey worth our while," he said. "There were other treasures in R'lin K'ren A'a. Come. . . ."

He led the way into the city.

Very few of the buildings were even partially standing, but they were nonetheless fascinating if only for the peculiar nature of their building materials, which were of a kind the travelers had never seen before.

The colors were many, but faded by time—soft reds and yellows and blues—and they flowed together to make almost infinite combinations.

Elric reached out to touch one wall and was surprised at the cool feel of the smooth material. It was neither stone nor wood nor metal. Perhaps it had been brought here from another plane?

He tried to visualize the city as it had been before it was deserted. The streets had been wide, there had been no surrounding wall, the houses had been low and built around large courtyards. If this was, indeed, the original

home of his people, what had happened to change them
from the peaceful citizens of R'lin K'ren A'a to the insane
builders of Imrryr's bizarre and dreaming towers? Elric
had thought he might find a solution to a mystery here,
but instead he had found another mystery. It was his fate,
he thought, shrugging to himself.

And then the first crystal disk hummed past his head
and smashed against a collapsing wall.

The next disk split the skull of a crewman and a third
nicked Smiorgan's ear before they had thrown themselves
flat among the rubble.

"They're vengeful, those creatures," Avan said with a
hard smile. "They'll risk much to pay us back for their
comrades' deaths!"

Terror was on the face of each surviving crewman and
fear had begun to creep into Avan's eyes.

More disks clattered nearby, but it was plain that the
party was temporarily out of sight of the reptiles. Smiorgan coughed as white dust rose from the rubble and
caught in his throat.

"You'd best summon those monstrous allies of yours
again, Elric."

Elric shook his head. "I cannot. My ally said he
would not serve me a second time." He looked to his left
where the four walls of a small house still stood. There
seemed to be no door, only a window.

"Then call something," Count Smiorgan said urgently.
"Anything."

"I am not sure. . . ."

Then Elric rolled over and sprang for the shelter, fling-
ing himself through the window to land on a pile of ma-
sonry that grazed his hands and knees.

He staggered upright. In the distance he could see the
huge blind statue of the god dominating the city. This was
said to be an image of Arioch—though it resembled no
image of Arioch Elric had ever seen manifested. Did
that image protect R'lin K'ren A'a—or did it threaten it?
Someone screamed. He glanced through the opening and
saw that a disk had landed and chopped through a man's
forearm.

He drew Stormbringer and raised it, facing the jade statue.

"Arioch!" he cried. "Arioch—aid me!"

Black light burst from the blade and it began to sing, as if joining in Elric's incantation.

"Arioch!"

Would the demon come? Often the patron of the kings of Melniboné refused to materialize, claiming that more urgent business called him—business concerning the eternal struggle between Law and Chaos.

"Arioch!"

Sword and man were now wreathed in a palpitating black mist and Elric's white face was flung back, seeming to writhe as the mist writhed.

"Arioch! I beg thee to aid me! It is Elric who calls thee!"

And then a voice reached his ears. It was a soft, purring, reasonable voice. It was a tender voice.

"Elric, I am fondest of thee. I love thee more than any other mortal—but aid thee I cannot—not yet."

Elric cried desperately: "Then we are doomed to perish here!"

"Thou canst escape this danger. Flee alone into the forest. Leave the others while thou hast time. Thou hast a destiny to fulfill elsewhere and elsewhen. . . ."

"I will not desert them."

"Thou art foolish, sweet Elric."

"Arioch—since Melniboné's founding thou hast aided her kings. Aid her last king this day!"

"I cannot dissipate my energies. A great struggle looms. And it would cost me much to return to R'lin K'ren A'a. Flee now. Thou shalt be saved. Only the others will die."

And then the Duke of Hell had gone. Elric sensed the passing of his presence. He frowned, fingering his belt pouch, trying to recall something he had once heard. Slowly, he resheathed the reluctant sword. Then there was a thump and Smiorgan stood panting before him.

"Well, is aid on the way?"

"I fear not." Elric shook his head in despair. "Once

again Arioch refuses me. Once again he speaks of a greater destiny—a need to conserve his strength."

"Your ancestors could have picked a more tractable
demon as their patron. Our reptilian friends are closing in.
Look. . . ." Smiorgan pointed to the outskirts of the city.
A band of about a dozen stilt-legged creatures were advancing, their huge clubs at the ready.

There was a scuffling noise from the rubble on the
other side of the wall and Avan appeared, leading his
men through the opening. He was cursing.

"No extra aid is coming, I fear," Elric told him.

The Vilmirian smiled grimly. "Then the monsters out
there knew more than did we!"

"It seems so."

"We'll have to try to hide from them," Smiorgan said
without much conviction. "We'd not survive a fight."

The little party left the ruined house and began to inch
its way through what cover it could find, moving gradually nearer to the center of the city and the statue of the
Jade Man.

A sharp hiss from behind them told them that the reptile warriors had sighted them again and another Vilmirian fell with a crystal disk protruding from his back.
They broke into a panicky run.

Ahead now was a red building of several stories which
still had its roof.

"In there!" Duke Avan shouted.

With some relief they dashed unhesitatingly up worn
steps and through a series of dusty passages until they
paused to catch their breath in a great, gloomy hall.

The hall was completely empty and a little light filtered through cracks in the wall.

"This place has lasted better than the others," Duke
Avan said. "I wonder what its function was. A fortress,
perhaps."

"They seem not to have been a warlike race," Smiorgan pointed out. "I suspect the building had some other
function."

The three surviving crewmen were looking fearfully

about them. They looked as if they would have preferred to have faced the reptile warriors outside.

Elric began to cross the floor and then paused as he saw something painted on the far wall.

Smiorgan saw it too. "What's that, friend Elric?"

Elric recognized the symbols as the written High Speech of old Melniboné, but it was subtly different and it took him a short time to decipher its meaning.

"Know you what it says, Elric?" Duke Avan murmured, joining them.

"Aye—but it's cryptic enough. It says: 'If thou hast come to slay me, then thou art welcome. If thou hast come without the means to awaken the Jade Man, then begone. . . .'"

"Is it addressed to us, I wonder," Avan mused, "or has it been there for a long while?"

Elric shrugged. "It could have been inscribed at any time during the past ten thousand years. . . ."

Smiorgan walked up to the wall and reached out to touch it. "I would say it was fairly recent," he said. "The paint still being wet."

Elric frowned. "Then there are inhabitants here still. Why do they not reveal themselves?"

"Could those reptiles out there be the denizens of R'lin K'ren A'a?" Avan said. "There is nothing in the legends that says they were humans who fled this place. . . ."

Elric's face clouded and he was about to make an angry reply when Smiorgan interrupted.

"Perhaps there is just one inhabitant. Is that what you are thinking, Elric? The Creature Doomed to Live? Those sentiments could be his. . . ."

Elric put his hands to his face and made no reply.

"Come," Avan said. "We've no time to debate on legends." He strode across the floor and entered another doorway, beginning to descend steps. As he reached the bottom they heard him gasp.

The others joined him and saw that he stood on the threshold of another hall. But this one was ankle-deep in fragments of stuff that had been thin leaves of a metallic material which had the flexibility of parchment. Around the walls were thousands of small holes, rank upon rank, each with a character painted over it.

"What is it?" Smiorgan asked.

Elric stooped and picked up one of the fragments. This had half a Melnibonéan character engraved on it. There had even been an attempt to obliterate this.

"It was a library," he said softly. "The library of my ancestors. Someone has tried to destroy it. These scrolls must have been virtually indestructible, yet a great deal of effort has gone into making them indecipherable." He kicked at the fragments. "Plainly our friend—or friends—is a consistent hater of learning."

"Plainly," Avan said bitterly. "Oh, the *value* of those scrolls to the scholar! All destroyed!"

Elric shrugged. "To Limbo with the scholar—their value to me was quite considerable!"

Smiorgan put a hand on his friend's arm and Elric shrugged it off. "I had hoped . . ."

Smiorgan cocked his bald head. "Those reptiles have followed us into the building, by the sound of it."

They heard the distant sound of strange footsteps in the passages behind them.

The little band of men moved as silently as they could through the ruined scrolls and crossed the hall until they entered another corridor which led sharply upward.

Then, suddenly, daylight was visible.

Elric peered ahead. "The corridor has collapsed ahead of us and is blocked, by the look of it. The roof has caved in and we may be able to escape through the hole."

They clambered upward over the fallen stones, glancing warily behind them for signs of their pursuers.

At last they emerged in the central square of the city. On the far sides of this square were placed the feet of the great statue, which now towered high above their heads.

Directly before them were two peculiar constructions which, unlike the rest of the buildings, were completely whole. They were domed and faceted and were made of some glasslike substance which defracted the rays of the sun.

From below they heard the reptile men advancing down the corridor.

"We'll seek shelter in the nearest of those domes," Elric said. He broke into a trot, leading the way.

The others followed him through the irregularly shaped opening at the base of the dome.

Once inside, however, they hesitated, shielding their eyes and blinking heavily as they tried to discern their way.

"It's like a maze of mirrors!" Smiorgan gasped. "By the gods, I've never seen a better. Was that its function, I wonder."

Corridors seemed to go off in all directions—yet they might be nothing more than reflections of the passage they were in. Cautiously Elric began to continue farther into the maze, the five others following him.

"This smells of sorcery to me," Smiorgan muttered as they advanced. "Have we been forced into a trap, I wonder."

Elric drew his sword. It murmured softly—almost querulously.

Everything shifted suddenly and the shapes of his companions grew dim.

"Smiorgan! Duke Avan!"

He heard voices murmuring, but they were not the voices of his friends.

"Count Smiorgan!"

But then the burly sea-lord faded away altogether and Elric was alone.

VI

He turned and a wall of red brilliance struck his eyes and blinded him.

He called out and his voice was turned into a dismal wail which mocked him.

He tried to move, but he could not tell whether he remained in the same spot or walked a dozen miles.

Now there was someone standing a few yards away, seemingly obscured by a screen of multicolored transparent gems. He stepped forward and made to dash away the screen, but it vanished and he stopped suddenly.

He looked on a face of infinite sorrow.

And the face was his own face, save that the man's coloring was normal and his hair was black.

"What are you?" Elric said thickly.

"I have had many names. One is Erekosë. I have been many men. Perhaps I am all men."

"But you are like me!"

"I am you."

"No!"

The phantom's eyes held tears as it stared in pity at Elric.

"Do not weep for me!" Elric roared. "I need no sympathy from you!"

"Perhaps I weep for myself, for I know our fate."

"And what is that?"

"You would not understand."

"Tell me."

"Ask your gods."

Elric raised his sword. Fiercely he said, "No—I'll have my answer from you!"

And the phantom faded away.

Elric shivered. Now the corridor was populated by a thousand such phantoms. Each murmured a different name. Each wore different clothes. But each had his face, if not his coloring.

"Begone!" he screamed. "Oh, Gods, what is this place?"

And at his command they disappeared.

"Elric?"

The albino whirled, sword ready. But it was Duke Avan Astran of Old Hrolmar. He touched his own face with trembling fingers, but said levelly, "I must tell you that I believe I am losing my sanity, Prince Elric. . . ."

"What have you seen?"

"Many things. I cannot describe them."

"Where are Smiorgan and the others?"

"Doubtless each went his separate way, as we did."

Elric raised Stormbringer and brought the blade crashing against a crystal wall. The Black Sword moaned, but the wall merely changed its position.

But through a gap now Elric saw ordinary daylight. "Come, Duke Avan—there is escape!"

Avan, dazed, followed him and they stepped out of the crystal and found themselves in the central square of R'lin K'ren A'a.

But there were noises. Carts and chariots moved about the square. Stalls were erected on one side. People moved peacefully about. And the Jade Man did not dominate the sky above the city. Here, there was no Jade Man at all.

Elric looked at the faces. They were the eldritch features of the folk of Melniboné. Yet these had a different cast to them which he could not at first define. Then he recognized what they had. It was tranquillity. He reached out his hand to touch one of the people.

"Tell me, friend, what year . . . ?"

But the man did not hear him. He walked by.

Elric tried to stop several of the passersby, but not one could see or hear him.

"How did they lose this peace?" Duke Avan asked wonderingly. "How did they become like you, Prince Elric?"

Elric almost snarled as he turned sharply to face the Vilmirian. "Be silent!"

Duke Avan shrugged. "Perhaps this is merely an illusion."

"Perhaps," Elric said sadly, "but I am sure this is how they lived—until the coming of the High Ones."

"You blame the gods, then?"

"I blame the despair that the gods brought."

Duke Avan nodded gravely. "I understand."

He turned back toward the great crystal and then stood listening. "Do you hear that voice, Prince Elric? What is it saying?"

Elric heard the voice. It seemed to be coming from the

crystal. It was speaking the old tongue of Melniboné, but with a strange accent. "This way," it said. "This way."

Elric paused. "I have no liking to return there."

Avan said, "What choice have we?"

They stepped together through the entrance.

Again they were in the maze that could be one corridor or many and the voice was clearer. "Take two paces to your right," it instructed.

Avan glanced at Elric. "What was that?" Elric told him. "Shall we obey?" Avan asked.

"Aye." There was resignation in the albino's voice.

They took two paces to their right.

"Now four to your left," said the voice.

They took four paces to their left.

"Now one forward."

They emerged into the ruined square of R'lin K'ren A'a. Smiorgan and one Vilmirian crewman stood there.

"Where are the others?" Avan demanded.

"Ask him," Smiorgan said wearily, gesturing with the sword in his right hand.

They stared at the man who was either an albino or a leper. He was completely naked and he bore a distinct likeness to Elric. At first Elric thought this was another phantom, but then he saw that there were also several differences in their faces. There was something sticking from the man's side, just above the third rib. With a shock, Elric recognized it as the broken shaft of a Vilmirian arrow.

The naked man nodded. "Aye—the arrow found its mark. But it could not slay me, for I am J'osui C'reln Reyr. . . ."

"You believe yourself to be the Creature Doomed to Live," Elric murmured.

"I am he." The man gave a bitter smile. "Do you think I try to deceive you?"

Elric glanced at the arrow shaft and then shook his head.

"You are ten thousand years old?" Avan stared at him.

"What does he say?" asked J'osui C'reln Reyr of Elric. Elric translated.

"Is that all it has been?" The man sighed. Then he looked intently at Elric. "You are of my race?"

"It seems so."

"Of what family?"

"Of the royal line."

"Then you have come at last. I, too, am of that line."

"I believe you."

"I notice that the Olab seek you."

"The Olab?"

"Those primitives with the clubs."

"Aye. We encountered them on our journey upriver."

"I will lead you to safety. Come."

Elric allowed J'osui C'reln Reyr to take them across the square to where part of a tottering wall still stood. The man then lifted a flagstone and showed them the steps leading down into darkness. They followed him, descending cautiously as he caused the flagstone to lower itself above their heads. And then they found themselves in a room lit by crude oil lamps. Save for a bed of dried grasses the room was empty.

"You live sparely," Elric said.

"I have need for nothing else. My head is sufficiently furnished. . . ."

"Where do the Olab come from?" Elric asked.

"They are but recently arrived in these parts. Scarcely a thousand years ago—or perhaps half that time—they came from farther upriver after some quarrel with another tribe. They do not usually come to the island. You must have killed many of them for them to wish you such harm."

"We killed many."

J'osui C'reln Reyr gestured at the others who were staring at him in some discomfort. "And these? Primitives, also, eh? They are not of our folk."

"There are few of our folk left."

"What does he say?" Duke Avan asked.

"He says that those reptile warriors are called the Olab," Elric told him.

"And was it these Olab who stole the Jade Man's eyes?"

When Elric translated the question the Creature Doomed to Live was astonished. "Did you not know, then?"

"Know what?"

"Why, you have been *in* the Jade Man's eyes! Those great crystals in which you wandered—that is what they are!"

VII

When Elric offered this information to Duke Avan, the Vilmirian burst into laughter. He flung his head back and roared with mirth while the others looked gloomily on. The cloud that had fallen across his features of late suddenly cleared and he became again the man whom Elric had first met.

Smiorgan was the next to smile and even Elric acknowledged the irony of what had happened to them.

"Those crystals fell from his face like tears soon after the High Ones departed," continued J'osui C'reln Reyr.

"So the High Ones did come here."

"Aye—the Jade Man brought the message and all the folk departed, having made their bargain with him."

"The Jade Man was not built by your people?"

"The Jade Man is Duke Arioch of Hell. He strode from the forest one day and stood in the square and told the people what was to come about—that our city lay at the center of some particular configuration and that it was only there that the Lords of the Higher Worlds could meet."

"And the bargain?"

"In return for their city, our royal line might in the future increase their power with Arioch as their patron. He would give them great knowledge and the means to build a new city elsewhere."

"And they accepted this bargain without question?"

"There was little choice, kinsman."

Elric lowered his eyes to regard the dusty floor. "And thus they were corrupted," he murmured.

"Only I refused to accept the pact. I did not wish to leave this city and I mistrusted Arioch. When all others set off down the river, I remained here—where we are now—and I heard the Lords of the Higher Worlds arrive and I heard them speak, laying down the rules under which Law and Chaos would fight thereafter. When they had gone, I emerged. But Arioch—the Jade Man—was still here. He looked down on me through his crystal eyes and he cursed me. When that was done the crystals fell and landed where you now see them. Arioch's spirit departed, but his jade image was left behind."

"And you still retain all memory of what transpired between the Lords of Law and Chaos?"

"That is my doom."

"Perhaps your fate was less harsh than that which befell those who left," Elric said quietly. "I am the last inheritor of that particular doom. . . ."

J'osui C'reln Reyr looked puzzled and then he stared into Elric's eyes and an expression of pity crossed his face. "I had not thought there was a worse fate—but now I believe there might be. . . ."

Elric said urgently, "Ease my soul, at least. I must know what passed between the High Lords in those days. I must understand the nature of my existence—as you, at least, understand yours. Tell me, I beg you!"

J'osui C'reln Reyr frowned and he stared deeply into Elric's eyes. "Do you not know all my story, then?"

"Is there more?"

"I can only *remember* what passed between the High Lords—but when I try to tell my knowledge aloud or try to write it down, I cannot. . . ."

Elric grasped the man's shoulder. "You must try! You must try!"

"I know that I cannot."

Seeing the torture in Elric's face, Smiorgan came up to him. "What is it, Elric?"

Elric's hand clutched his head. "Our journey has been

useless." Unconsciously he used the old Melnibonéan tongue.

"It need not be," said J'osui C'reln Reyr. "For me, at least." He paused. "Tell me, how did you find this city? Was there a map?"

Elric produced the map. "This one."

"Aye, that is the one. Many centuries ago I put it into a casket which I placed in a small trunk. I launched the trunk into the river, hoping that it would follow my people and they would know what it was."

"The casket was found in Melniboné, but no one had bothered to open it," Elric explained. "That will give you an idea of what happened to the folk who left here. . . ."

The strange man nodded gravely. "And was there still a seal upon the map?"

"There was. I have it."

"An image of one of the manifestations of Arioch, embedded in a small ruby?"

"Aye. I thought I recognized the image, but I could not place it."

"The Image in the Gem," murmured J'osui C'reln Reyr. "As I prayed, it has returned—borne by one of the royal line!"

"What is its significance?"

Smiorgan interrupted. "Will this fellow help us to escape, Elric? We are becoming somewhat impatient. . . ."

"Wait," the albino said. "I will tell you everything later."

"The Image in the Gem could be the instrument of my release," said the Creature Doomed to Live. "If he who possesses it is of the royal line, then he can command the Jade Man."

"But why did you not use it?"

"Because of the curse that was put on me. I had the power to command, but not to summon the demon. It was a joke, I understand, of the High Lords."

Elric saw bitter sadness in the eyes of J'osui C'reln Reyr. He looked at the white, naked flesh and the white hair and the body that was neither old nor young, at the shaft of the arrow sticking out above the third rib on the left side.

"What must I do?" he asked.

"You must summon Arioch and then you must command him to enter his body again and recover his eyes so that he may see to walk away from R'lin K'ren A'a."

"And when he walks away?"

"The curse goes with him."

Elric was thoughtful. If he did summon Arioch—who was plainly reluctant to come—and then commanded him to do something he did not wish to do, he stood the chance of making an enemy of that powerful, if unpredictable entity. Yet they were trapped here by the Olab warriors, with no means of escaping them. If the Jade Man walked, the Olab would almost certainly flee and there would be time to get back to the ship and reach the sea. He explained everything to his companions. Both Smiorgan and Avan looked dubious and the remaining Vilmirian crewman looked positively terrified.

"I must do it," Elric decided, "for the sake of this man. I must call Arioch and lift the doom that is on R'lin K'ren A'a."

"And bring a greater doom to us!" Duke Avan said, putting his hand automatically upon his sword-hilt. "No. I think we should take our chances with the Olab. Leave this man—he is mad—he raves. Let's be on our way."

"Go if you choose," Elric said. "But I will stay with the Creature Doomed to Live."

"Then you will stay here forever. You cannot believe his story!"

"But I do believe it."

"You must come with us. Your sword will help. Without it, the Olab will certainly destroy us."

"You saw that Stormbringer has little effect against the Olab."

"And yet it has some. Do not desert me, Elric!"

"I am not deserting you. I must summon Arioch. That summoning will be to your benefit, if not to mine."

"I am unconvinced."

"It was my sorcery you wanted on this venture. Now you shall have my sorcery."

Avan backed away. He seemed to fear something more than the Olab, more than the summoning. He seemed to read a threat in Elric's face of which even Elric was unaware.

"We must go outside," said J'osui C'reln Reyr. "We must stand beneath the Jade Man."

"And when this is done," Elric asked suddenly, "how will we leave R'lin K'ren A'a?"

"There is a boat. It has no provisions, but much of the city's treasure is on it. It lies at the west end of the island."

"That is some comfort," Elric said. "And you could not use it yourself?"

"I could not leave."

"Is that part of the curse?"

"Aye—the curse of my timidity."

"Timidity has kept you here ten thousand years?"

"Aye. . . ."

They left the chamber and went out into the square. Night had fallen and a huge moon was in the sky. From where Elric stood it seemed to frame the Jade Man's sightless head like a halo. It was completely silent. Elric took the Image in the Gem from his pouch and held it between the forefinger and thumb of his left hand. With his right he drew Stormbringer. Avan, Smiorgan, and the Vilmirian crewman fell back.

He stared up at the huge jade legs, the genitals, the torso, the arms, the head, and he raised his sword in both hands and screamed:

"*Arioch!*"

Stormbringer's voice almost drowned his. It pulled in his hands; it threatened to leave his grasp altogether as it howled.

"*Arioch!*"

All the watchers saw now was the throbbing, radiant sword, the white face and hands of the albino and his crimson eyes glaring through the blackness.

"*Arioch!*"

And then a voice which was not Arioch's came to Elric's ears and it seemed that the sword itself spoke.

"Elric—Arioch must have blood and souls. Blood and souls, my lord. . . ."

"No. These are my friends and the Olab cannot be harmed by Stormbringer. Arioch must come without the blood, without the souls."

"Only those can summon him for certain!" said a voice, more clearly now. It was sardonic and it seemed to come from behind him. He turned, but there was nothing there.

He saw Duke Avan's nervous face, and as his eyes fixed on the Vilmirian's countenance, the sword swung around, twisting against Elric's grip, and plunging toward the duke.

"No!" cried Elric. "Stop!"

But Stormbringer would not stop until it had plunged deep into Duke Avan's heart and quenched its thirst. The crewman stood transfixed as he watched his master die.

Duke Avan writhed. "Elric! What treachery do you . . . ?" He screamed. "Ah, no!"

He jerked. "Please . . ."

He quivered. "My soul . . ."

He died.

Elric withdrew the sword and cut the crewman down as he ran to his master's aid. The action had been without thought.

"Now Arioch has his blood and his souls," he said coldly. "Let Arioch come!"

Smiorgan and the Creature Doomed to Live had retreated, staring at the possessed Elric in horror. The albino's face was cruel.

"Let Arioch come!"

"I am here, Elric."

Elric whirled and saw that something stood in the shadow of the statue's legs—a shadow within a shadow.

"Arioch—thou must return to this manifestation and make it leave R'lin K'ren A'a forever."

"I do not choose to, Elric."

"Then I must command thee, Duke Arioch."

"Command? Only he who possesses the Image in the Gem may command Arioch—and then only once."

"I have the Image in the Gem." Elric held up the tiny object. "See."

The shadow within a shadow swirled for a moment as if in anger.

"If I obey your command, you will set in motion a chain of events which you might not desire," Arioch said, speaking suddenly in Low Melnibonéan as if to give extra gravity to his words.

"Then let it be. I command you to enter the Jade Man and pick up its eyes so that it might walk again. Then I command you to leave here and take the curse of the High Ones with you."

Arioch replied, "When the Jade Man ceases to guard the place where the High Ones meet, then the great struggle of the Upper Worlds begins on this plane."

"I command thee, Arioch. Go into the Jade Man!"

"You are an obstinate creature, Elric."

"Go!" Elric raised Stormbringer. It seemed to sing in monstrous glee and it seemed at that moment to be more powerful than Arioch himself, more powerful than all the Lords of the Higher Worlds.

The ground shook. Fire suddenly blazed around the form of the great statue. The shadow within a shadow disappeared.

And the Jade Man stooped.

Its great bulk bent over Elric and its hands reached past him and it groped for the two crystals that lay on the ground. Then it found them and took one in each hand, straightening its back.

Elric stumbled toward the far corner of the square where Smiorgan and J'osui C'reln Reyr already crouched in terror.

A fierce light now blazed from the Jade Man's eyes and the jade lips parted.

"It is done, Elric!" said a huge voice.

J'osui C'reln Reyr began to sob.

"Then go, Arioch."

"I go. The curse is lifted from R'lin K'ren A'a and

from J'osui C'reln Reyr—but a greater curse now lies upon your whole plane."

"What is this, Arioch? Explain yourself!" Elric cried.

"Soon you will have your explanation. Farewell!"

The enormous legs of jade moved suddenly and in a single step had cleared the ruins and had begun to crash through the jungle. In a moment the Jade Man had disappeared.

Then the Creature Doomed to Live laughed. It was a strange joy that he voiced. Smiorgan blocked his ears.

"And now!" shouted J'osui C'reln Reyr. "Now your blade must take my life. I can die at last!"

Elric passed his hand across his face. He had hardly been aware of any of the recent events. "No," he said in a dazed tone. "I cannot. . . ."

And Stormbringer flew from his hand—flew to the body of the Creature Doomed to Live and buried itself in its chest.

And as he died, J'osui C'reln Reyr laughed. He fell to the ground and his lips moved. A whisper came from them. Elric stepped nearer to hear.

"The sword has my knowledge now. My burden has left me."

The eyes closed.

J'osui C'reln Reyr's ten-thousand-year life-span had ended.

Weakly, Elric withdrew Stormbringer and sheathed it. He stared down at the body of the Creature Doomed to Live and then he looked up, questioningly, at Smiorgan.

The burly sea-lord turned away.

The sun began to rise. Gray dawn came. Elric watched the corpse of J'osui C'reln Reyr turn to powder that was stirred by the wind and mixed with the dust of the ruins. He walked back across the square to where Duke Avan's twisted body lay and he fell to his knees beside it.

"You were warned, Duke Avan Astran of Old Hrolmar, that ill befell those who linked their fortunes with Elric of Melniboné. But you thought otherwise. Now you know." With a sigh he got to his feet.

Smiorgan stood beside him. The sun was now touching the taller parts of the ruins. Smiorgan reached out and gripped his friend's shoulder.

"The Olab have vanished. I think they've had their fill of sorcery."

"Another man has been destroyed by me, Smiorgan. Am I forever to be tied to this cursed sword? I must discover a way to rid myself of it or my heavy conscience will bear me down so that I cannot rise at all."

Smiorgan cleared his throat, but was otherwise silent.

"I will lay Duke Avan to rest," Elric said. "You go back to where we left the ship and tell the men that we come."

Smiorgan began to stride across the square toward the east.

Elric tenderly picked up the body of Duke Avan and went toward the opposite side of the square, to the underground room where the Creature Doomed to Live had lived out his life for ten thousand years.

It seemed so unreal to Elric now, but he knew that it had not been a dream, for the Jade Man had gone. His tracks could be seen through the jungle. Whole clumps of trees had been flattened.

He reached the place and descended the stairs and laid Duke Avan down on the bed of dried grasses. Then he took the duke's dagger and, for want of anything else, dipped it in the duke's blood and wrote on the wall above the corpse:

This was Duke Avan Astran of Old Hrolmar. He explored the world and brought much knowledge and treasure back to Vilmir, his land. He dreamed and became lost in the dream of another and so died. He enriched the Young Kingdoms—and thus encouraged another dream. He died so that the Creature Doomed to Live might die, as he desired. . . .

Elric paused. Then he threw down the dagger. He could not justify his own feelings of guilt by composing a high-sounding epitaph for the man he had slain.

He stood there, breathing heavily, then once again picked up the dagger.

He died because Elric of Melniboné desired a peace and a knowledge he could never find. He died by the Black Sword.

Outside in the middle of the square, at noon, still lay the lonely body of the last Vilmirian crewman. Nobody had known his name. Nobody felt grief for him or tried to compose an epitaph for him. The dead Vilmirian had died for no high purpose, followed no fabulous dream. Even in death his body would fulfill no function. On this island there was no carrion to feed. In the dust of the city there was no earth to fertilize.

Elric came back into the square and saw the body. For a moment, to Elric it symbolized everything that had transpired here and would transpire later.

"There is no purpose," he murmured.

Perhaps his remote ancestors had, after all, realized that, but had not cared. It had taken the Jade Man to make them care and then go mad in their anguish. The knowledge had caused them to close their minds to much.

"Elric!"

It was Smiorgan returning. Elric looked up.

"The Olab dealt with the crew and the ship before they came after us. They're all slain. The boat is destroyed."

Elric remembered something the Creature Doomed to Live had told him. "There is another boat," he said. "On the east side of the island."

It took them the rest of the day and all of that night to discover where J'osui C'reln Reyr had hidden his boat. They pulled it down to the water in the diffused light of the morning and they inspected it.

"It's a sturdy boat," said Count Smiorgan approvingly. "By the look of it, it's made of that same strange material we saw in the library of R'lin K'ren A'a." He climbed in and searched through the lockers.

Elric was staring back at the city, thinking of a man who might have become his friend, just as Count Smiorgan had become his friend. He had no friends, save Cymoril, in Melniboné. He sighed.

Smiorgan had opened several lockers and was grinning at what he saw there. "Pray the gods I return safe to the Purple Towns—we have what I sought! Look, Elric! Treasure! We have benefited from this venture, after all!"

"Aye. . . ." Elric's mind was on other things. He forced himself to think of more practical matters. "But the jewels will not feed us, Count Smiorgan," he said. "It will be a long journey home."

"Home?" Count Smiorgan straightened his great back, a bunch of necklaces in either fist. "Melniboné?"

"The Young Kingdoms. You offered to guest me in your house, as I recall."

"For the rest of your life, if you wish. You saved my life, friend Elric—now you have helped me save my honor."

"These past events have not disturbed you? You saw what my blade can do—to friends as well as enemies."

"We do not brood, we of the Purple Towns," said Count Smiorgan seriously. "And we are not fickle in our friendships. You know an anguish, Prince Elric, that I'll never feel—never understand—but I have already given you my trust. Why should I take it away again? That is not how we are taught to behave in the Purple Towns." Count Smiorgan brushed at his black beard and he winked. "I saw some cases of provisions among the wreckage of Avan's schooner. We'll sail around the island and pick them up."

Elric tried to shake the black mood from himself, but it was hard, for he had slain a man who had trusted him, and Smiorgan's talk of trust only made the guilt heavier.

Together they launched the boat into the weed-thick water and Elric looked back once more at the silent forest and a shiver passed through him. He thought of all the hopes he had entertained on the journey upriver and he cursed himself for a fool.

He tried to think back, to work out how he had come to be in this place, but too much of the past was confused with those singularly graphic dreams to which he was

prone. Had Saxif D'Aan and the world of the blue sun
been real? Even now, it faded. Was this place real? There
was something dreamlike about it. It seemed to him he had
sailed on many fateful seas since he had fled from
Pikarayd. Now the promise of the peace of the Purple
Towns was very dear to him.

Soon the time must come when he must return to
Cymoril and the Dreaming City, to decide if he was ready
to take up the responsibilities of the Bright Empire of
Melniboné, but until that moment he would guest with
his new friend, Smiorgan, and learn the ways of the
simpler, more direct folk of Menii.

As they raised the sail and began to move with the
current, Elric said to Smiorgan suddenly, "You trust me,
then, Count Smiorgan?"

The sea-lord was a little surprised by the directness of
the question. He fingered his beard. "Aye," he said at
length, "as a man. But we live in cynical times, Prince
Elric. Even the gods have lost their innocence, have they
not?"

Elric was puzzled. "Do you think that I shall ever be-
tray you—as—as I betrayed Avan, back there?"

Smiorgan shook his head. "It's not in my nature to
speculate upon such matters. You are loyal, Prince Elric.
You feign cynicism, yet I think I've rarely met a man so
much in need of a little real cynicism." He smiled. "Your
sword betrayed you, did it not?"

"To serve me, I suppose."

"Aye. There's the irony of it. Man may trust man,
Prince Elric, but perhaps we'll never have a truly sane
world until men learn to trust mankind. That would mean
the death of magic, I think."

And it seemed to Elric, then, that his runesword trembled at his side, and moaned very faintly, as if it were
disturbed by Count Smiorgan's words.